70 Days
—*with*—
Hugh Jackman

SANDY EVANSKI

Copyright © 2018 Sandy Evanski
All rights reserved
First Edition

PAGE PUBLISHING, INC.
New York, NY

First originally published by Page Publishing, Inc. 2018

This novel is a fictitious account of true events.

ISBN 978-1-64462-362-6 (Paperback)
ISBN 978-1-64462-363-3 (Digital)

Printed in the United States of America

~ Dedication ~

My brother Dr Jerry Evanski
You are the most caring, loving, and funny brother ever.
Thank you for your support and encouragement.
If anyone has any complaints about the
book please direct them to him.

CHAPTER 1

Hold On Tight

HUGH JACKMAN—ACTOR, AUSTRALIAN, Wolverine, beefcake, Oscar emcee, singer, and dancer, with a list of movie credits and accomplishments as long as your arm. He is a happily married and loving dad known to be generous to a fault and enormously loyal to the big three: family, friends, and fans; and I want to spend seventy days with him.

Now, who would ever believe a registered nurse (RN) set medic, with virtually no movie production experience, could land the gig of the century and spend seventy days with Hugh Jackman? How could a set medic, any set medic, land a gig like this and hang onto it? It would be as A. A. Freda said: hold on tight and fight as hard as you can. I remember the exact day I found out Hugh Jackman was coming to the home of Motown and the Automobile Capital of the World, Detroit, Michigan. Unfortunately, my beloved Detroit was on a downward spiral, financially filing for bankruptcy and jeopardizing our crown jewel, the Detroit Institute of Art (DIA).

CHAPTER 2

The Crown Jewel

THE DETROIT INSTITUTE of Art collection boasts of having one of the largest and most significant art collections in the nation. From the first painting donated in 1883 to its most recent acquisition, the collection of over sixty thousand works, have brought culture and creativity of the world to Detroit's doorstep. Ranging from classic to cutting-edge, the works housed in the DIA would challenge perceptions and enrich perspectives of anyone who viewed the collection. Once talk of selling the art collection to rescue the city of Detroit from bankruptcy began, it was difficult to keep the appraisers from Christie's out of our backyard; and believe me, my friend, if you think the art collection in your city will never be in jeopardy, think again. Once these debt collectors picked up the scent on how Detroit could rescue itself from bankruptcy, it was challenging to keep these bum bailiffs out of our town.

It was all everyone talked about, especially when the proposed estimate on the potential sale of the art collection could bring in $454 to $867 million! Fortunately, after a two-year court battle, a federal ruling to approve a bankruptcy plan brought an end to the threat to auction off the DIA's collection, mainly from a grand bargain of an eight-hundred-million-dollar deal, a miraculous deliverance from insolvency. The Ford, Knight, and Kresge foundations were the heavy hitters who rescued our art collection and the city of Detroit. Who could have ever known Detroit would go through a Renaissance period and come out swinging and looking better than ever? Detroit endured and proved it could do so much more.

CHAPTER 3

He's Coming to Detroit!

I BELIEVE IT WAS Amy Madigan's husband from the movie *Field of Dreams* who spoke the words, "If you build it, they will come," and were they ever, with no signs of slowing down. Now, in the middle of its great comeback story of Detroit's rebirth, buildings were being constructed, and new businesses moved into the city. Michigan sports leagues claimed home to new stadiums all within walking distance of downtown Detroit—the Lion's Ford Football Field, Tigers Baseball Comerica Park, and the newly constructed Little Caesar's Stadium for the Red Wings and Detroit Pistons. Not many cities can boast of these accomplishments. But how does any of this even relate to Hugh Jackman?

Months earlier, I read an article in our local newspaper, *The Detroit Free Press*, that the Australian *beefcake*, Hollywood megastar, and legend Hugh Jackman would be coming to the Motor City and star in a movie made in Michigan. Wait, who? Hugh Jackman, as in *the* Hugh Jackman? No way! Even as I said it out loud, I was filling up with a feeling of desperation and dread. I didn't care if I was a set medic neophyte, I wanted that gig. I uttered under my breath, "No one like me, with minimal set medic experience, would ever get close to getting this movie assignment, not even on special effects or working on postproduction cleanup." I knew what I didn't have in experience as a movie set medic I made up for in my forty years as a registered nurse. But the cold, hard fact was, even with my many years as a nurse, I knew my name was never going to be listed in the film credits as the set medic for production on a movie of this caliber.

I had started out so many years ago as a cashier and stocker for a grocery chain named A&P's. Remember them? The Great Atlantic and Pacific Tea Company. I can still smell the coffee beans I ground up for each customer while I rang up their groceries. I don't even drink coffee, but the smell of freshly ground coffee beans smelled like home sweet home. I also worked for several other grocery store chains. For $1.10 an hour, I rang up meat and Tide detergent at the Super Kmarts in Louisiana. I also worked at the Safeway grocery store in Las Vegas and got paid $6.35 an hour with every Wednesday and Sunday off.

It was all a means to an end. I knew I couldn't survive on the salary I was paid and make a decent living. So I worked nights and put myself through college earning my associate's degree in allied health, making me eligible to take my nursing state boards, and I passed! I was an RN, a registered nurse. My degree and results from the State Boards said so! I couldn't leave the grocery store business fast enough—all to earn $4.25 an hour working in a surgical ICU. Yes, $4.25 an hour. I couldn't wait to start my new career saving lives as an RN.

CHAPTER 4

Heads or Tails

I DISCOVERED MY LIFE'S passion over the flip of a coin. Heads, I would be a teacher; and tails, a nurse. Once my life's course was determined by the flip of a coin, no one could talk me out of it. What a rush to experience someone in cardiac distress and know exactly what to do. I would compress their chest with my hands and breathe my oxygen into their lungs, saving their lives. No fancy equipment, just me. I thought, *What would I be able to do with medical supplies and equipment at my beck and call?* I was hooked! For the rest of my life, I lived to save lives. I worked nights in a surgical ICU and completed my bachelor of science in nursing. Time marched on, and I discovered nurses were never going to receive the recognition we richly deserved in spite of our education and willingness to work weekends, holidays, back-to-back double shifts, with no breaks or dedicated time to eat lunch, at least not for many years to come.

Nurses administered medications, IV antibiotics, changed dressings, and monitored vital signs around the clock. Due diligence and assessment skills of a nurse notifying doctors in a timely fashion have saved many lives. Forty years later, having worked in ICUs, emergency rooms, cardiac step-down units, general and surgical care unit, and ambulatory clinics, I continued to perfect my nursing skills every day. My newest goal was to figure out a way to land the movie gig of a lifetime as a nurse set medic, the person everyone contacted on a movie set when cast, crew, or an extra were injured and required medical help. The movie Hugh Jackman was going to star in wasn't scheduled to begin production for months, so I put the project in the back of my mind but never took my eye off the prize. I kept working as a set medic in any capacity, on any movie that came my way. It didn't matter if it was production, working with special effects, or a postproduction crew. Every experience as a nurse set medic was like being a nurse for the first time. There was so much to learn, and I found every movie I worked on, I learned something new. No two movies, like patients, were ever alike.

CHAPTER 5

Was I Ready?

I HAVE NEVER BEEN a stranger to figuring out how to make something happen in my life, and working in the movie industry was no different. I have found over the years it isn't what you know but who you know. Never underestimate the importance of one's network of personal contacts. You never know when they would come in handy. Now, the tax incentives being offered by Michigan was a powerful catnip to dangle in front of the moviemakers from Los Angeles who were always on the prowl for ways to save money. Seeing all the action coming out of LA was my signal to put together a résumé showcasing my many years as an RN and send it to the local stagehands union, IATSE, and wait.

    I was excited at the prospect of working on a movie set. A cherry job! I would be working with hundreds of skilled craftsmen, highly paid actors, directors, and producers. What could go wrong? My days as a nurse were filled with anything from emergent tracheostomies, GI bleeds, bowel obstructions, pain control, drain and wound care, high blood pressure, diarrhea, administering chemotherapy, radiation therapy, pain management, women who thought they were in active labor and ready to deliver to women who thought they were in active labor but weren't even pregnant. Anything you could think of and then some. No matter what the outcome, I was ready to be a set medic in the movies.

CHAPTER 6

Red Dawn

GETTING INTO THE movie industry wasn't easy. I waited six weeks after sending in my résumé before I received *the call*. I had just hit the snooze bar when my phone rang. No one I knew would call me this early on my day off. There was one reason, and one reason only, my phone was ringing this early. I knew this was the call! I could feel it deep in my bones. A male voice on the other end of the phone asked if I was a set medic and if I wanted to work on a remake of the movie *Red Dawn*.

"Sure!" I squeaked back at him. "Yes, I would!"

"Do you have your own jump kit?" he asked.

"My own what? A jump what? Yes, of course, I do! All of the medics have jumpers—jump sets," I said, cringing.

The male voice continued. "We've had a lot of eye injuries, flash burns. Do you have anything in your jump kit to treat that with?"

"Yes, yes, I do." I had just told a big white lie. In truth, I didn't have anything ready. "When do you need me?"

"Three hours ago!" he growled. "When can you be here?"

"Soon! Really, really, really soon," I assured him. First thing's first, I needed to find something to carry medical supplies. I found an old backpack and headed off to the medicine cabinet, emptying the contents into my bag. What should I bring? Normal saline, eye drops, alcohol, hydrogen peroxide, gauze pads, several rolls of gauze, one- and two-inch tapes, cough syrup—no, put the cough syrup back. No one is going to have a cold. I packed Steri-Strips, Vaseline, Benadryl strips, condoms... Condoms? Where did those come from? Hmm, tampons... I don't need those anymore. *Well, someone could have a nosebleed*, I thought and threw them in. I was dressed at the speed of sound and out the door.

Not really certain where I was going to end up, I entered the address into my GPS. The adrenaline rush at the very thought of working on a real movie set was an overwhelming incentive to ignore my speedometer and drive like I was transporting a loved one to the ER with crushing chest pain. Wow. The remake of *Red Dawn*. I never saw the original, but I remembered Patrick Swayze starred in it. Maybe he would be a consultant on the movie? I arrived at the address and brought my van to a screeching halt.

CHAPTER 7

You're Late!

I ENTERED THE BUILDING, backpack slung over my shoulder filled with medical supplies, and stopped short. I stood there on the spot, looking dumbfounded. There were no movie actors or cherry pickers with directors holding a megaphone yelling, "Action!" No sign of Patrick Swayze. I was looking into a warehouse filled with equipment, work tables, dust, and workers sawing, drilling, and pounding away at multiple different projects in all different stages of completion. Wow, did I ever feel out of place.

"Hi!" I said, locking eyes with the first person walking toward me. "I'm your set medic." As soon as I said it, I knew I said it too loud. He motioned with his head toward the front of the building to a man sitting behind a desk with staplers, White-Out, Scotch tape, and piles of paper in front of him. Who was this guy? Well, it turned out he was the most important man in the room, the purchasing agent. He was responsible for purchasing materials and supplies needed to build the scenery and props for a movie. The purchasing agent was a "who you know" person. He could cut deals on supplies with the local vendors and find supplies no one else knew how to locate. In the movie industry, you would find yourself in a different state and location every few months. It was helpful to have someone with a little black book filled with names and phone numbers of those in the industry who kept the supplies coming in for the Special

Effects crews to build what was needed in time for the production of a movie. He looked up at me then looked at the clock on the wall then back at me in an accusing tone.

"Hey!" I said. "I just got the call and got here as soon as I could. I know I'm late."

"Put your jump kit over there," he said without blinking an eye. "The other medic is out with the explosion team and won't be back until six. The backup medic who's supposed to be here has called in again! We work 6 AM–6 PM Monday through Friday. You want this job?"

"Yeah! I mean, yes," I stuttered, turning red. "I'll be here, sir!"

He grinned over his pile of paperwork in front of him and said, "All right then. Drop off your gear and come back to fill out your paperwork. Let's get to work!"

I dropped my off my *jump kit*, returning to fill out the paperwork making me officially the set medic with the Special Effects team for the remake of *Red Dawn*. My paperwork completed, the purchasing agent introduced me to some of the crew and said, "On Fridays, we deep-fry Amish turkeys for five bucks a head if you want in."

"Sounds—"

I was cut off with him turning and walking away and saying, "Okay, if you need anything, call me. In the meantime, just be ready."

"For what?" I asked innocently.

He turned around and looked me and said, "Anything!"

CHAPTER 8

Always Prepared

JUST THE TONE of his voice made me reach into my pocket and feel for my exam gloves. Old habits die hard. I have been caught with my pants down around my ankles one too many times over my nursing career. I've had patients throw up on me without a formal introduction, disconnected IVs leaking solution over everything in its path, or confused patients pulling out their IV lines out, leaving a trail of blood everywhere. I had learned the hard way from hundreds of different scenarios to always keep a pair of exam gloves on me at all times. I carried exam gloves in my pocket at work, home, church, and dance recitals. If Ryan Seacrest asked me on the red carpet whose designer dress I was wearing and what I had in my diamond-encrusted evening bag, I would open it and reveal to two hundred countries around the world viewing the Academy Awards a pair of exam gloves staring back at them.

But back to Special Effects. What a group of hardworking, skilled craftsmen. Carpenters, electricians, painters, and welders all working at various stages, building the sets and props for a movie scene. Quality was not an option but an expectation. And don't think about calling in sick. Call in if you're feeling brave, but you would be taking a big chance on Hollywood calling in another skilled craftsman to replace you. The movie industry is not hurting for skilled professionals waiting to get their big break. You learn how to *suck it up* and figure out a way to make it through the day, or be replaced at the snap of a finger. You pick.

Several weeks went by, and before I was actually feeling comfortable at my new job, there were hours and hours of downtime. No one was injured, and filling in the hours became a new adventure for me. I reviewed and restocked my jump kit, a term that I found out meant the medic's medical supply kit. Walking around the building was good exercise, but the heat from the warm Michigan summer made me yearn to be back in the warehouse where it was somewhat cooler, with a gentle breeze wafting through the building. I explored the local restaurants on my lunch hour and enjoyed the deep-fried Amish turkeys on Fridays. Life was good.

CHAPTER 9

Sting Like a Bee

I HAD ALMOST BECOME complacent about why I was even at the warehouse daily when close to quitting time on a Friday afternoon, there was a bloodcurdling scream heard above the drilling, sawing, and welding. It only took me a moment to snap on my gloves, zip open my backpack, and look in the direction of the screams heading my way. What was the emergency? I couldn't see who was screaming. Then it revealed itself.

One of the carpenters working with a power saw was running toward me with his hands covered in blood. Blood was everywhere, streaked across his face, and all over his clothes. Bright-red blood was spurting, not flowing, out from under his grasp. The blood was spurting so forcefully it hit me in my cheek with such force it felt like a bee had stung me. There was no mystery here. He had cut an artery, and I only had precious minutes to get it under control. I grabbed a handful of four-by-fours and followed the stream of the pulsating blood back down to the source. I calmly turned to a crew member and said, "Call 911. Tell them an employee severed an artery in his hand, and we need an ambulance. Stat! Go now!"

The rest of the warehouse was quiet. All you could hear was the quiet whimpering from the wounded man. He kept looking at me pleadingly with his eyes to just make it right. I applied firm pressure on the bleeding site, but blood continued to seep out from under the four-by-fours in spite of my best attempts to stop it. I knew this was a catastrophic hemorrhage requiring emergent intervention. I had to apply a tourniquet that would cut off the blood supply to the area for small increments of time. The pressure I was giving just wasn't good enough. He had already lost so much blood. However, using a tourniquet is very dangerous. Not used correctly, it can result in nerve damage, tissue death, and blood clots, to name just a few contraindications. But there was no time for second-guessing. I turned to the crew member closest to me and said, "Take off your belt. Go on, do it!" He just stared at me. "Now!" I commanded, and he finally jolted into action. "Now, put the belt above the wound and tighten it like you're going to buckle it. Yes, keep going. Don't stop." I could feel the pulsating of the artery beneath my fingers finally slowing down, and just in time. My hand was cramping so badly. I kept instructing my new assistant to keep the belt right where it was and changed out the four-by-fours. I watched the time on my watch. It was critical not to keep the tourniquet on for too long. It was imperative to keep oxygen-rich blood circulating to the area as important as it was to decrease the loss of blood. In the distance I could hear the wailing of a siren from the fast-approaching ambulance. Thank God!

Finally, the medics arrived and came crashing through the door. They had already been notified of the grave situation and didn't waste a minute starting an IV and administering IV fluids. You have to love the beautiful, big, firm veins of a twenty-year-old. When I worked in the ER and needed to start an IV, or draw blood on a younger person, I didn't even use a tourniquet. I just asked them to make a fist, and veins would pop out everywhere. I was grateful for this young man's age, and getting the IV lines started without difficulty was critical. Vital signs were taken as I kept tightening and releasing the grip of the tourniquet. The medics kept in constant communication with their home base hospital, continuing to keep the ER staff updated. Time was our enemy. Surgical intervention to repair the artery was imperative. So many things could go wrong: infection, tetanus, compartment syndrome, nerve damage, even loss of the hand; the list was endless. Finally, we all agreed. With the IV lines in place and the tourniquet controlling the bleeding, it was time to transport to the

ER. Ordinarily, two medics would transport the patient, but an extra pair of hands in this case was mandatory to manage the tourniquet. I jumped into the back of the rig, and we left. Seven minutes was our ETA, or our expected time of arrival.

I remember asking many times in the late seventies, while riding in Rescue 14 in Las Vegas, going out on regular runs with the paramedics, "What is our ETA?" I was lucky to be a part of a program allowing RNs who worked in the ER to take turns rotating out on the field with the medics. The experiences were invaluable. I witnessed so much action and learned very quickly how dangerous being a medic out in the field could be. The medics did everything. They delivered babies, managed heart attacks, drowning victims, sexual assaults, smoke inhalation, and did crisis intervention. All this and walking in on situations without any protection from knife-wielding assailants, guns going off, drunks throwing punches, and delirious patients from drug overdoses. Riding with the medics, to this day, is still one of the best experiences I have had in my nursing career. I always remember the base operator asking when we were finally on the road, "Medic, what's your ETA?" Our ETA was seven minutes. An eternity seemed shorter. I continued to monitor how long the tourniquet cut off the blood supply to the area and then releasing the tourniquet so that oxygen-rich blood would flow back to the traumatized tissue.

At long last, we arrived at the ER. The doors on the back of the rig flew open to a sea of waiting doctors and nurses. They escorted the stretcher to a waiting bay area. Initially they weren't happy to see I had utilized a tourniquet made out of a belt, but once they removed the four-by-fours, the entire tone of the room changed. No one needed to say anything more once they assessed the severed artery and the acute loss of blood. Wordlessly, the tourniquet stayed in place. A hospital gown replaced the blood-drenched clothes being cut off. IV pain medication given, the patient typed and cross-matched for a blood transfusion. How many transfusions he would need, I just didn't know. But it was going to be a lot. Then the patient was whisked off to surgery. The bay area was a disaster. Open packages, needles, bloody clothes, electrode pads, and empty IV bags littered the floor. I've seen this scenario thousands of times. *What a mess,* I thought, walking through it. I had enough respect for everything strewn around to know I would never get tired of looking at it. This mess was a measure of the heroic actions taken moments earlier by a truly gifted team of ER personnel dedicated to saving lives. I walked through the doors of the ER to a calm, still night. The air smelled so clean. I found a driver from transportation waiting for me.

"Come on," he said. "I'll drive you back to the warehouse."

CHAPTER 10

RN Set Medic

EVERYTHING HAD BEEN cleaned up at the warehouse when I arrived. My report needed to be written and turned in. Everyone except for the purchasing agent was still there.

"Whoa! Pretty fast moving, eh?" he said.

"You know it!" I replied.

"Will he be okay?" he asked.

"I'm not 100 percent certain, but he has a pretty good chance of not losing his hand. We transported him to a world-class trauma center. One of the best in Michigan. The ER and surgical team were waiting for him when we arrived. He's in surgery now. I'll stop off and see him tomorrow. Let me finish up this report, and let's get out of here. I'm beat!"

The rest of my time with the Special Effects team went by pretty smoothly compared to the traumatic night we had that Friday afternoon. I treated eye abrasions, pulled out slivers, wrapped sprained wrists, dressed smashed thumbs from misdirected hammer swings, and gave out a fair share of Band-Aids. The next thing I knew, six weeks had gone by, and the job was a wrap. The good news was I had made it through. The purchasing agent made me the best going-away present, an ID badge dressing me as a red-caped superwoman. I looked awesome, and under my name was "RN/Medic"! What a head rush. I actually had made it through my first gig.

After *Red Dawn*, the jobs came effortlessly. There were so many movies being made in Michigan, a complement to our beautiful state with many natural resources. Unfortunately, because of the financially challenging time, many Michiganders, like so many others across the country, were out of work. I did a few more gigs with Special Effects crews and worked postproductions restoring location sites to their original state. I even scored a few gigs working on production, small movies, but they allowed me expanded exposure to the movie industry. I really enjoyed getting to know the crew, learning about their jobs, and how they each contributed to the outcome of a movie.

No wonder ticket prices are so expensive. In the past, after I had seen a movie, I would get up and leave. Now, I sit and look at all the credits and pay close attention to the hundreds of names of skilled professionals utilized to make a movie. I always paid special attention to who the set medics were for production and Special Effects. I would sit back and try to imagine what type of medical emergencies they may have encountered during the production of a movie. I felt the same way about being a set medic. I was shaky at first (that was a given), figuring out where to stand or what to do with extra time on my hands. How to pack my jump kit with the right supplies for the job? I was still a nurse, but I was learning how to do it in a new way. I was very confident with my clinical skills and relieved to know I could assess and move just as fast as I needed to in a crisis situation. It was like riding a bike. Skills nurtured for so many years never go away. You just do it without any thought. It comes so naturally. I also learned how to enhance my presence as a set medic. During the cold and flu season, I put out bottles of hand sanitizers, encouraged frequent handwashing, and made boxes of Kleenex readily available. I also provided packets of Airborne to everyone on the crew. I put signs up around the set to remind people to promote good health and made a habit of serving up a big Crock-Pot full of chicken noodle soup on chilly evenings when we filmed night scenes. Everyone on the set seemed to enjoy the extra effort I put out. The French call it *Lagniappe*, or to give something extra. For all my extra efforts, I was assigned to be the medic on more films, giving me the boost of confidence I needed.

CHAPTER 11

Circling the Campfire

SINCE MY LAST movie, I had gone for a month without a gig. Summer was coming, and there was nonstop talk about the movies being made in Michigan. Forty-five- to sixty-day shoots were the talk around the watercoolers. Months had gone by since I had seen the announcement that Hugh Jackman was going to star in a movie made in Detroit. I quietly inquired if anyone knew when the preproduction crew was arriving. Turned out, everyone had taken an interest in the movie starring Hugh Jackman. Gosh, just saying Hugh Jackman was going to be starring in a movie made in Michigan was so cool, and Detroit was looking good. I also discovered there wasn't a set medic in a two-hundred-mile radius who wasn't interested in getting this production gig. All the set medics were circling the fire, and my chances of getting this movie were slim to none. I had to face reality, having little experience on the production end of movie as a medic. I had about fifteen movie credits to my name, and most of them were working postproduction. All I felt was futility, like climbing a StairMaster and never getting anywhere.

Several weeks later, I heard the preproduction crew had arrived. There was so much hustle and bustle in a preproduction office. You could feel the excitement in the air. The preproduction crew always came into town weeks in advance of the actual start of the production of a movie. Paperwork was being created, and payroll, established. A mountain of questions was being peppered at the preproduction crew. Who do we call for transportation? What time is catering arriving? Why is one actor arriving before the other? Are we able to accommodate the director's family and have private nannies available when they arrive for their children? Who will be the schoolteachers for the actors still in school? There are books of rules and regulations guiding the movie industry in hiring and directing child actors. Which hotel are the key crew members staying in? When are they arriving? Is the Special Effects crew on schedule? Which IATSE office was the contact? Hundreds of questions were filtered through the preproduction office, and eventually, all questions were answered.

Me? I was shameless! I had nothing to lose by picking up the phone and calling the preproduction office three to four times a day. I left my name, phone number, and purpose of my call every time. "I'm interested in being the set medic for your movie, special effects or production." It didn't matter. The answer was always the same, "Leave your information, and we will get back to you." *Sure*, I thought. *Answer my call and five hundred more like it.* My attempts seemed futile. Honestly, why was I even bothering? I just had an itch needing to be scratched. It was a cold, hard fact I was delirious with determination to land this gig! I had to keep calling and asking no matter what the outcome. At least I knew I would have tried my best. The last week of preproduction, and I had resigned myself to accepting any available movie in the area. The writing was on the wall—set medics with years of experience were going to get the job!

Heavy sigh!

CHAPTER 12

Area Code (248)

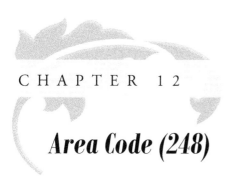

THEN MY LUCK changed, and I felt the slightest breeze of hope blowing in my direction. I received a phone call displaying a (248) area code on the last Friday prior to the onset of production, late in the afternoon on my coverless cellphone taped together with black electric tape, securing the battery from falling out. I honestly just sat there staring at the (248) area code that could only mean one thing. This was the area code for the production company for Hugh's movie. And they were calling me.

"Hello?" *Calm down, calm down*, I said to myself silently.

The voice on the other end said, "Could I speak with Sandy, please?"

"This is she. How can I help you?"

The voice continued, "I'm with the preproduction company for the movie Hugh Jackman is starring in. Production begins Monday, and we are in need of an ambulance to be on the set for a week. We called your union, and they recommended we contact you. You're a nurse, correct?"

"Yes, yes. I'm an RN set medic. What can I do for you?"

"I was hoping you would be able to locate an ambulance company and arrange for them to be on location with us the first week of production," the voice continued.

"Ambulance? Of course. It would be my pleasure to obtain the information for you in about fifteen minutes?"

"Yes, of course," she replied. "Now, may I give you my office and cellphone numbers so you and I can stay in touch? It's rather important I have all this arranged before the end of the workday." I thought, *I would have the office* and *cellphone numbers of the one person who held the outcome of my life for the next seventy days!*

I assured her I would call her back and went to work! The possibility of being involved with Hugh Jackman was enough to satisfy even the most crazed medic attempting to get this gig. I desperately wanted to be involved. The clock was ticking. I called three ambulance companies in the area and asked for prices and availability with medics. Each company seemed as excited as I was when I explained why I needed the information. I typed my research up on Word and called the assistant back at the production company in record time. When she answered she sounded so surprised. "You have the answer already?" she said in disbelief.

"Why, yes. Yes, I do," I said, rather matter-of-factly. "Where would you like the information faxed too?" She gave me the fax number and was in the process of thanking me for all my work when I just blurted out, "Have you hired the set medic for the movie yet?" I just sat there on the other end of the line with the ends of the electric tape curling up over the corners of my coverless flip phone. It felt like an eternity before she replied.

"Do you want special effects or production?"

"Production," I whispered back very quietly. As soon as I uttered the ten-letter word, I knew I had gotten the job. My eyes were actually swelling up with tears. My hands were shaking. I felt like I had been transported to another time. She didn't waste a minute giving me instructions.

"Be here before 7:00 tonight to fill out paperwork and get your picture ID. Bring a copy of your résumé and driver's license. Don't be late. Production starts at 7:00 AM sharp on Monday. It's a seventy-day shoot. No cameras or filming equipment of any kind. No smoking on the set."

"Yes, ma'am. I understand. I'll be right there."

"Oh, and one more thing," she added. "Do you have your own jump kit?"

I smiled back into the phone and answered, "Yes, I have a jump kit!" I sat there staring at the phone when the call ended.

What did I just accomplish? What in the world just happened here? One hour ago, I expected to get a phone call saying, "Thank you for your many calls, but we've hired the set medic for this production. So please, stop calling our office four times a day." I just wanted to be able to say I had at least tried to get any job doing anything with this movie. I would be turned down, but at least I tried!

Now I was just holding my taped-up coverless cell phone and began to cry uncontrollably! Every part of my body was shaking! I couldn't stop smiling through the tears. I grabbed my purse and ran to my van and sped at the speed of sound to the production office. I felt like Bette Midler was singing "I'm the Wings Beneath Your Feet." I had just won the golden ticket of the century with pure dumb luck. I landed the ungettable gig! I was the official set medic on production for a seventy-day shoot with a huge, mega movie star. I was going to spend the next seventy days with Hugh Jackman.

CHAPTER 13

Stop or I'll Shoot!

"MOST PEOPLE'S HINDSIGHT is 20-20," was attributed to humorist Richard Armour, and I was no different. The address for the call site on Monday morning directed me to a wheat field fifty miles from where I lived and would be a long drive home after twelve to sixteen-hour production days. But I knew in my heart of hearts this would all be worth it, a small price to pay to work with Hugh Jackman. But a wheat field?

Over the months, I had accumulated an extensive collection of medical supplies. I literally was ready for anything to happen. I may have only been a medic on a dozen or so movies, but I was a quick study. I learned quickly what I needed for the crews and made my way with five totes brimming with medical supplies with everything and anything a nurse could think of. Rain the night before created mud puddles, wet grass, and sticking wheat sheaths clinging to my shoes with every step I took. *Good lord*, I thought, *am I ever going to get to the main entrance?*

Finally approaching the main gate, a security officer greeted me. I flashed him my badge and was continuing to walk onto the property when he yelled, "Stop!"

"Stop?" I thought to myself, *Why do I need to stop?* The officer approached me suspiciously.

"I need to inspect your totes and see what you are bringing in here." I looked at him in total disbelief.

"I'm the set medic. All I have are medical supplies."

"Well, let's just see," he said, removing the lids from my totes and inspecting the contents. What did he expect to find? Paparazzi? Really? "Okay. You're clear to go," he said authoritatively. He grabbed his radio and said, "Security 1 to main gate. Medic has arrived, and I have inspected her gear. She's clear."

I'm what? What kind of production site is this? I said to myself silently. I made the next part of the journey over long pieces of plywood laid over big areas of mud puddles. What a mess, with mosquitoes—the Michigan State bird—nibbling at my ankles while I struggled with my cart. Finally, I arrived at my destination, pleasantly surprised to see a midway constructed with cheesy fixed games, a variety of rides featuring the graviton, food trucks with candy apples, elephant ears, sweet and salty popcorn, pizza rolls, and cold lemonade.

I kept my badge in clear view with security everywhere. Everyone kept eyeing me and my cart full of medical supplies. I kept smiling and looking back at them. Once in a while I would say, "Set medic. These are the medical supplies!"

Finally, a security guard approached me. "Follow me. I'll show you where you can set up," he said, leading me to the opposite side of the fairgrounds, past a dirt-covered arena where a corral had been constructed. *What was the corral supposed to be keeping in?* I thought. No one had said anything about a corral and a grandstand that could easily accommodate a thousand people.

CHAPTER 14

No Bulling Around

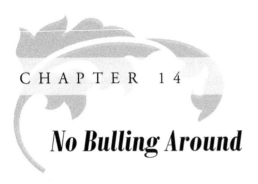

I WAS STARTING TO get a bad feeling but didn't have time to think about it because the ambulance arrived and was backing up to the medic station. I was hired at the last minute, never having an opportunity to read the script and know what to expect or why we needed ambulance backup the next five days. The movies I worked on in production had a number of people on the set but not to this extent, leading me to be more concerned. After setting up my station, I wandered over to the corral, spotting a horse trailer where a group of cowboys, some dressed like clowns, were sitting on bales of hay. I knew one of America's most popular homegrown sports is the rodeo, where cowboys pit their skill and endurance against bucking broncos and bulls. It's dangerous work, and injuries among bull riders, in particular, are common. But they would be in greater danger without the clowns, also called bullfighters, who distract the beasts and allow the riders to escape injury if thrown off the back of a raging bull.

"Hi, guys. I'm Sandy, your set medic."

One of the bullfighters replied quickly, "Oh, little lady, we don't need a set medic. We take care of our own injuries."

"You what?"

"No worrying about us. We take care of our own injuries. This isn't our first rodeo," the bullfighter reiterated.

"Not your first rodeo," I repeated. "You take care of your own injuries? Exactly what kind of injuries are you talking about?"

They all laughed at me, and the bullfighter said, "Come with me and meet Big John."

You mean like Big from Sex and the City, I thought. He led me to a concealed fenced in area. The fence was at least twelve feet high with a viewing window built in.

"Come here," he directed. "Look," he directed, pointing his finger to the viewing window. *Oh my god!* I thought, looking through the window. Staring back at me was a four-thousand-pound bull, a big black bull with horns nearly a foot long. And not only Big John, but also his buddies, the Terminator and Son of Sam. I looked back at the bullfighter in total disbelief.

"Oh no," I said. "Not bulls!" I grew up on a farm and was terrified of them. My dad borrowed a bull from a different neighbor every time our cow needed to be bred. Sometimes we even traveled to the next county to find a bull for the cow. The brotherhood of the bull was, once a cow had been serviced by him, she was no longer "new cow," and the bull would have nothing more to do with her. Now the bull referred to her as "old cow." *Well*, I thought, *not much separating the bull from man's world*. We kept the bull tied up until he was turned loose with the cow and got the job done.

Now staring back at me was the biggest bull I had ever seen in my life, snorting and looking like he had a bigger migraine than the one I was getting. The bullfighter / rodeo clown was getting a kick out of my insecurity around the bull.

"Don't worry." He continued, "We have been around these bulls for a long time. We're used to them."

"Be honest with me. What's the worst-case scenario?" I asked.

The bullfighter / rodeo clown replied, "Well, if a man gets caught under the hooves of a four-thousand-pound bull, he can be crushed in an instant," paraphrasing the comment by snapping his fingers in front of my face. He continued. "The bull's horns are treacherous. They can grow to more than a foot in length and can cause internal injury if you don't get out of their way fast enough.

Don't worry. You're only in grave danger if the horn happens to strike a vital organ like your heart or your lungs," he said nonchalantly.

Right about then, the medics from the ambulance showed up. I introduced myself and asked the rodeo clown if he would do the honors of introducing Big John to them. I barely had time to absorb the information about the bulls when my radio started talking to me.

CHAPTER 15

Talk to Me, Baby!

"MEDIC, MEDIC, MEDIC. Channel 3!" my radio commanded. *Okay, okay!* I thought to myself, replying, "Medic on 3."

"What's your location?" The voice on the radio demanded.

"I'm by the bull pen. What's your location, and I'll meet you," I responded. I grabbed my backpack and met security on the opposite side of the arena. There were six men waiting for me. *My, my, my. I'm popular today*, I thought. "Guys, what's up?" They rolled back their sleeves, pulled their shirts up to their chest, and pulled up their pant legs. They were covered in hundreds of bug bites. Inspecting the bites closer, I said, "It looks like some bedbugs had a food fest last night. Are all of you sleeping in the same hotel?"

"Yes," one of the men offered. "We flew in from LA late last night. Transportation took us directly to the hotel. When we got up this morning we were covered with these bites. Can you help us?" he said, pointing to the inflamed, edematous, itchy skin.

"Yes, but it's going to take a bit to get this under control. We aren't exactly in an environment to encourage healing. After we wrap tonight, go back to your hotel and take cool showers. Hot water will enhance the production of histamine, which will cause you to itch, so keep it cool and try to keep the affected areas as dry as possible. Bugs love to set up housekeeping in warm, moist, dark areas. Don't give them any reason to get comfortable.

"I'm going to encourage each and every one of you to work on bringing out your feminine side. After you shower, I want you to gently pat your skin dry with a soft towel. Seriously, be gentle. You've been bitten and your skin is very inflamed and swollen. I'll have security call the hotel manager and have your mattresses all traded out for new ones and request the carpets be cleaned and treated before you get back or, at the very least, relocate all of you to rooms which have already been treated." They all just stood still looking at me like I had just told them they had to work for free.

"What?" I said. "I'm not kidding. Do exactly what I just told you. I also want each and every one of you, unless you have a medical reason, to start taking Motrin every eight hours along with a Tylenol. The Motrin will help to ease the inflammation, and the Tylenol will help with any localized pain from the excoriated areas from itching. Then apply this hydrocortisone cream to the bitten areas, and before going to bed, take a 25 mg Benadryl, which will help stop the reaction of the histamine making you itch. And no drinking! Give the Benadryl a half of a chance to work.

"Listen to me, and you'll start feeling better soon. If there isn't any improvement in the next two days, we'll have a doctor brought to the set. Okay, now give me your names so I can file an incident report to get the hotel rooms cleaned to my satisfaction. Also, get your suitcases up off the floor and put them into the bathtub. Don't leave any of your clothes lying on the floor, especially your underwear, unless you want me to apply cream to your butts and whatnots!" They all grinned and lined up. I doled out steroid cream by the tube along with a generous supply of Motrin, Tylenol, and Benadryl to each crew member.

"Okay," I said, satisfied. "Now, report back to me in the morning and see how well you're doing. Now, don't bother me anymore today. This is all the time I have for you," I said, grinning back at them. "Go! Get back to work. We cannot make a movie without any of you!"

CHAPTER 16

No Drugs for Sale

I HEADED BACK TO the medic station and immediately saw a disturbing sight—a sea of extras was heading my way from makeup and wardrobe stations. They started filling up the empty stadium, and I took advantage of the situation. I took an available mic and made the following announcement: "I'm Sandy, your set medic. If you need me for any medical reason, ask one of the PAs [production assistants] to contact me, and I will come and see you. I'm a medic, not a doctor. I do not carry drugs of any kind with me. I cannot get drugs of any kind, and I don't know of anyone who will get you any drugs you think you need. The only medications, and I mean the only medications, I have are Motrin and Tylenol. So if you need something stronger for a headache, upset stomach, heartburn, asthma, hay fever, sore throat, high blood sugar, monthly cramps, or antibiotics for an infection, bring it in yourself. If you came to work without your medication, report to the PA, and they will excuse you for the day. This is not a hospital. It's a movie set. And I repeat, I'm a medic, not a doctor. Any questions?"

Someone yelled out, asking if I had drugs, and everyone laughed. "No more announcements from me! Have a fun day!" I said back.

The extras all started talking amongst themselves again. The mood was lighthearted. The first day of production is always fun, just the excitement of meeting new people. Working as an extra, you were paid eighty dollars a day and fed three meals on top of the chance to be seen in the final movie cut. If you were lucky enough to be an extra, you were just lucky enough!

CHAPTER 17

Gaffers, Key Grips, and Best Boys, Oh My!

MY RADIO STARTED yelling at me again. "Medic, Medic, Medic! What's your location?"

I thought to myself, *Did you not just hear me speaking over a mic to over a thousand extras in the arena?*

"Medic on 3. I'm in the arena. What's your location?"

"It's security. I have one of the gaffers with me. Meet me at your station."

"On my way. Over and out!" One of the most interesting revelations to me were all the names given to the crew. I actually had to sit down and write them out as I learned them.

The gaffer is known as the chief lighting technician. He works with the director of photography for developing a lighting plan for the movie. He will also communicate with the key grip and the best boy, who is the lead electrician, on where the lights will be placed during the filming of the movie. The key grip, who is the lead grip, is also in charge of all the grips. The grips build and provide everything being built around the lights to create the quality of light the gaffer is requesting. The key grip also oversees proper camera-rigging mechanisms as well as managing the light blocking and diffusing techniques.

Right now I had a gaffer waiting for me at my station whom I recognized right away. We had worked together on a movie several months earlier. God, he had the bluest eyes I had ever seen in my life! We both shared a feeling of mutual admiration. I pictured him thinking back about me, *This medic has the most medical supplies I have ever seen in my life!* Anyway, he had his usual complaint; his ankles and feet were killing him. If he were one of the extras, I would have sent him to security and had him sent home. But he was a crew member, and I prided myself on taking very good care of the crew. They never ever received anything generic, only the best of the best.

"Well, friend, this is your lucky day," I said to him. "I had a hunch our paths would cross again, so I already purchased and brought along with me new shoe inserts, ankle supports, and your own supply of Motrin and Tylenol. I see you did buy a really nice pair of work shoes," I said, admiring his new footwear.

"Yeah, but even with the new boots, my ankles and feet are really talking to me."

"Well, let's get you squared away!" And I went to work on his feet and ankles, working my magic. I applied a pain-relieving cream, wrapped ace wraps around his feet and ankles, and gave him a generous supply of Tylenol and Motrin, sending him on his way.

Overhead, I could hear the PAs giving instructions to the extras. No, wait. That was the director's voice I heard. Oh no, we're starting to film! The extras were instructed on a signal from the director to yell as though they were watching two Roman centurions fighting to the death. The extras started to scream at the director's signal as though their lives depended on it. The director was thrilled.

"Great!" he directed back. "Keep going, don't stop! Louder!" The extras obliged, taking their yelling and screaming to a level I didn't think was possible. This director was great. He really knew how to get what he wanted out of a group of extras.

"Medic, Medic, Medic! What's your location?" my radio demanded from me.

"I'm by my station. Where's your emergency?" I answered over the screaming.

Over and over again through the morning, the calls never stopped coming in, wave after wave of calls. The first day on this set for medical emergencies was brutal, and the heat and humidity were unforgiving.

CHAPTER 18

Who Was That?

THE DAY MARCHED on when, just out of the corner of my eye, I saw him. Just for a microsecond, and there he was again! It was Hugh! It was such a head rush to see him for the first time. I couldn't help but notice how tall he was, and he was wearing a red kerchief around his neck. He was smiling and walking toward the back of the arena with the director, with a huge group of people around him all vying for his attention at the same time. It was like watching a group of two-year-olds all trying to get their mother's attention at the same time, *Listen to me* or *Talk to me*. He had an electric aura about him that just drew you into him. Whoa, even from the distance I was from him, I just wanted to be by him, not even talking to him, but just be near him.

I had been so busy all morning long I had forgotten he was going to be there. Now out of nowhere, here he was and headed right for the bull pen. No, no, no, no, no! I ran after him. I knew the rodeo clowns were okay on their own, but not Hugh. Don't let him anywhere near those bulls. Although if I had ever worked with Hugh before, I would have known this was Hugh just being Hugh. He just had to check the bulls out, and the director was giving him the grand tour! Then, in the next minute, he was gone, swallowed up by the masses. But the rush of just seeing him so close just took your breath away! For the moment, this was just going to have to be enough.

CHAPTER 19

The Mysterious Blonde

"MEDIC, MEDIC, MEDIC!" my radio was blaring at me.

"What?" I yelled back at the radio. "Medic on 3, what's your emergency?"

"It's security. We're out of bug spray!" *And that's my problem why?* I thought out loud.

"I'll handle it and get back to you ASAP." I took out my coverless taped-up cellphone and was in the middle of calling the local pharmacy to deliver several cases of bug spray and sunscreen to the set when a woman's angry and demanding voice spoke directly to me from behind.

"Do you want to continue working on this movie?" I spun around and came face-to-face with a beautiful, tan, slim, early-middle-aged woman staring back at me. She kept staring at me and repeated, "I said, do you want to continue working on this movie?" Her voice was cold, curt, and full of meaning. I was so startled I just stood there staring at her. I couldn't speak. My mouth was moving, but nothing was coming out. I could tell nothing less than complete respect was the only way to behave.

"Yes, ma'am, I do. I like working here! I want to keep my job!" I said. She just kept looking at me while the pharmacist from the drugstore on the end of my phone was jabbering on about where to deliver the bug spray and sunscreen.

"Bug spray...," I said out loud and offered my phone to her at the same time. "I'm ordering bug spray and sunscreen. It will be delivered to the set within the hour." I kept holding my phone out toward her to show her the innocence of my phone call.

She kept staring at me and finally said, "You know there is no picture-taking on this movie?"

"Yes, ma'am!" I replied instantly. "I signed a statement of understanding when I reported to preproduction for my badge." I held my badge up to her so she could see I even had a badge, as if someone could even get on this set without one. "My cellphone doesn't even have a camera. See?"

She kept staring at me sternly and said, "Have everything delivered to security up front. Turn in your receipts for anything you purchase up and above the daily reimbursement for your jump kit to Finance, and you will be reimbursed. Understand?" Not waiting for an answer, she just walked away.

I just stared at her disappearing silhouette. Frozen in my tracks, I was shaking like a leaf! Who was she? I had endured eight years of nuns at Catholic grade school, and nothing came close to how this woman could make you feel. I still couldn't shake the feeling security was going to show up at any time to escort me off the set. My god! Who was she? For now, she had to remain a mystery!

CHAPTER 20

You Are Too Sweet!

I WENT ABOUT COLLECTING myself and completed ordering the bug spray and sunscreen when my radio blared as if on cue. "Medic, Medic, Medic! What's your location?" I thought to myself, *Good lord! No rest for the wicked, weary, and nearly fired medic!*

"Medic on 3. I'm by my station. What's your location?" I replied.

"It's security. We are under the bleachers on the south side of the fairgrounds. We have a crew member down. We need you stat!"

Gloves flying on, I raced toward the location. I arrived at the scene and found the crew member sitting on the ground. He was conscious but shaky, clammy, diaphoretic, and dizzy. He was holding his right arm out for me to see. He was clearly tattooed down the length of his arm from his elbow down to the wrist; in big blue lettering, the word DIABETIC. I took out my glucometer and pricked his finger. Within a minute, the meter read thirty-nine. I brought out a tube of glucagon gel and said, "Swallow this," squeezing it into his mouth. "Swallow!" He was still able to follow commands.

I remained calm and focused. A group of people started to congregate and watched the scenario unfolding in front of them. Turning to security, I said, "Run and get some orange juice from Crafty services." Then turning to the second security officer, I said, "Move this crowd back. Ask them to return to their jobs. No gawking." Security arrived with the orange juice. His hands were trembling handing me the glass. I said, "He's going to be okay. Just breathe!" He smiled back. I pricked the diabetic's finger again, and the glucometer read fifty. Good! We were making progress. The patient was calmer, dryer, and more awake. Handing him the orange juice I said, "Drink this. Now!" He started sipping the juice slowly. I turned to security and said, "Okay, give me ten more minutes, and I'll take another reading. Then we'll have transportation take him to the local urgent care center." Security arrived shortly after with a wheelchair, while I was rechecking the blood sugar again—sixty-one. Yes! My patient was very much awake now and repeated what I had just said, "Sixty-one." Thank God!

"Hey, where did you go?" I said. He smiled a bit. "Okay, partner, I know you've been through this drill before, but you really took a nosedive. Just as a safety measure, transport is going to take you to the local urgent care center. I want the doctor to check you out to make sure your blood sugar is stable before you come back to work. But you're done for today. Here. I've prepared a report for the doctor so they know everything that happened and the treatment I gave you. When you report for work in the morning, check in with me first thing. Okay?" He nodded in agreement and kept drinking his juice. As security wheeled the patient away, I thought to myself, *I really dodged a bullet there!* Just then, a raindrop landed on the tip of my nose.

CHAPTER 21

Rain, Rain, Go Away!

I WAS SO BUSY getting my diabetic's sugar to a safe level I didn't notice a big cloud cover had moved in. I hoped this was just an isolated drop. But on a day like today? The way my luck was going? Oh no, no, no, no, my friend. This would be a happy ending. Just then, as if on cue, the skies opened up, and an unrelenting, drenching rain started to fall. I ran back to my station and threw lids back on the totes filled with medical supplies. My hair was sticking unmercifully to my face. I couldn't see out of my glasses. Every bone in my body was screaming to be let out of this hole of unending heat, humidity, rain, and never-ending calls coming over the radio. And it was only 11:30 AM! The rain let up after ten minutes and reduced itself to a fine, annoying drizzle. Then an announcement came over the radio, "Break for lunch. Everyone report back at 1:00 PM."

I limped back to my station and pulled out a big red backpack and walked over to the ladies' room, which was air-conditioned! The irony of it all. Are you kidding me? I stripped off my wet clothes and stood there in my private little stall in the air-conditioned ladies' room and started to laugh hysterically. With tears falling down my cheeks and laughter that just wouldn't stop, this day was going to go down as the worst possible first day in set medic history. *No one would believe this*, I thought. No one would ever believe so much pain and mystery could happen so fast in the few first working hours on a new movie—starring Hugh Jackman, no less. I brushed my hair back into a ponytail and wiped myself dry. I kept a backpack with a change of clothes just for a moment like this. Everything was dry: the towel, underwear, new set of clothes, and even socks and tennis shoes. By the time I emerged from the ladies' room, I was a new person with half an hour to eat lunch. I looked down at my radio, which I never turned off, ever. Then I said a silent prayer to it to keep quiet for just the next thirty minutes so I could eat my lunch in peace and quiet. Compared to the challenging morning I had, my radio graciously behaved itself the rest of the afternoon with fewer calls.

CHAPTER 22

Don't Tease Me, or I'll Gore You!

THE UNFORGIVABLE HUMIDITY and heat continued on throughout the afternoon with rain gusts sprinkled here and there. The day did get a lot easier once I enlisted the help of my ambulance colleagues. Technically, not set medics, but being a trained health care professional was the only important requirement. The afternoon labored on, and I continued to catch a glimpse of Hugh here and there. However, the scenes filmed after lunch were the bullfighters teasing Big John to charge after them. He was snorting and digging his hooves into the dirt. He was *massive* and frightening to watch. He would charge after the bullfighter rodeo clown at such speed and viciousness. But every time, and I mean every time, one of the rodeo clowns managed to get Big John or any of the other bulls to charge after them, they avoided being gored by successfully climbing up the side of the corral fence and lifting their legs high into the air as the bull climbed up the fence behind them.

Toward the end of the day, one of the cowboys anticipating Big John was too tired to climb up the fence after he let his guard down and didn't climb up the fence fast enough. So Big John helped him up the side of the corral fence with his horns. It wasn't pleasant to watch, and the reaction of the crowd was an attestation to how painful it must have been to have a one-foot horn running up the back of your quads and into your backside. The rodeo cowboys who inspected the wound kept assuring me it was "nothing" and wouldn't let me even look at it. Finally, after much persuasion, the cowboy agreed to have his leg bandaged with just plain-white cloth tape. But he wouldn't let me examine him. He would only agree to let the EMT from the ambulance crew look at the wound and bandage him in the privacy of the ambulance. *Perhaps,* I thought, *those cowboys are just shy around women*? The EMT reassured me one roll of four-inch white cloth tape later. The wound was more like a graze up his quad and barely nicked his glutes. He allowed the EMT to clean the wound and apply the tape. This was all he would agree to do. No four-by-four gauze pads, no abdominal pads, nothing. Just *terrible* white cloth tape.

Near the end of filming, around 6:00 PM, the clouds had cleared. The humidity lightened just a bit, and a warm westerly breeze replaced the scorching heat and unrelenting humidity. My clothes were sticking to every orifice of my body and screaming for a cool, clean shower. Thankfully, the extras were released to go home with a call time for seven AM. I replenished my medic totes and took inventory of everything I had and what I needed to purchase before returning in the morning. I had stockpiled supplies in bulk I kept in the back of my van so I wouldn't have to make a trip every night to a local pharmacy. Task completed and released by the head PA, I headed for home in my van with a nonworking air conditioner and windows that no longer rolled up and down. If I stopped too long at a traffic light, the engine warning light would blink on, and the overheat engine light would illuminate. My baby drank two cans of oil a day. But on the plus side, the radio worked, tires were all new, and if I held the driver's door open just a little while I was driving, I could get a nice breeze going through the cabin long enough to stay cool. Unfortunately, there was no room in the budget for a new or used van at this juncture. This one was just going to have to do for now. Thank God it was summer. The thought of this bad boy breaking down in the middle of an icy snowstorm wasn't anything I ever wanted to endure.

I headed for home in my hot van with the driver's door wedged open to let a breeze in. The police would pull me over from time to time to ask me if everything was okay, observing my door opened with my foot. Within an hour, I was pulling into my driveway. Home sweet home. The overheat engine gauge was starting to rise as I pulled into my driveway. I dragged my weary body into the house, peeling off my wet clothes, leaving a trail of mud and muck behind me. I stood frozen under the cool water cascading over me in the shower forever. I didn't want to move! What a day. I just wanted to forget my first day on this movie. I went to bed and fell asleep instantly. I closed my eyes for just a second, and the alarm started to buzz. I sat up in bed in the dark totally, disoriented for a minute. Where was I? Why was the alarm going off? Had I missed the first day of filming with Hugh? But the minute I started to move my body, the harsh memories from the day before came rushing back at me, and I remembered with a shiver how terrible it had been. Crawling out of bed, I took another warm shower to loosen my joints and asked forgiveness one more time from my body for the torture I had put it through the day before. As always, she forgave me. She wouldn't forget, but she forgave me.

CHAPTER 23

Pull Up a Chair and Eat!

I GOT INTO MY van in the coolness of the morning hours and headed off for day two of seventy days with Hugh Jackman. What a difference a day makes. When I arrived on the set, things went much more smoothly. Security still insisted on frisking me at the main gate, but to be honest, I rather enjoyed it. Those security guards from LA were really bulked up and cute!

After my morning frisking, I headed off to the food tent for breakfast. I truly believe the movie industry heeded the advice of Harvard-educated poet, Witter Bynner, pen name Emmanuel Morgan, in his 1929 collection of poems published in Indian Earth: "For the spirits of men, the more they eat, have happier hands and lighter feet."

If there is one thing the movie industry does correctly, it's that they feed their crew great food! Even on a movie with a small budget, attention is given to the food services company hired to feed the crew.

Eggs were cooked the way you wanted, bacon, ham, sausage, and hash brown potatoes tumbling over the tops of serving pans; hot black coffee with a variety of creamers or an eclectic collection of different teas, if that's what you preferred; every type of juice you could imagine: pineapple, orange, grape, mango, and tomato. I think the movie industry's motto is "A happy well-fed crew equals a well-made movie!" No sooner had breakfast been cleared away when Crafty services would kick it up a notch, setting out tables of food to hold us over until lunch. Bagels, muffins, nuts, a cornucopia of fruits, vegetables, crackers, chips, coffee, tea, water, juices, flavored seltzer waters—it went on and on. Then an hour away from lunch, Crafty services provided several six-foot subs, a tray full of sandwiches, or a collection of meat and crackers to complement the food already set out. No one could ever say they didn't have enough to eat while filming a movie. The remaining two meals were met with as great of a fanfare as breakfast. Catering had delicious, hot meals, and the desserts were amazing. They had ice cream, cookies, cakes, pies, and decorative trifle. But breakfast was over, and it was time to report for duty. My radio, turned on from the minute I arrived and before I endured my morning frisking, was set on channel 3, so far remaining quiet!

I wandered over to the main tent where the directors, producers, and actors hung out. No one was there yet, but on their arrival, a major hug fest ensued, accompanied by all sorts of courteous pleasantries every day: "Good Morning!" "Did you sleep well last night?" "Was your driver on time?" Every morning, the same scenario while I watched from the distance. Hmm, I wonder what it would be like if the doctors I worked with in the hospital just came up and gave *me* a hug, asked *me* how I slept last night and if my van got *me* into work on time. I am such a dreamer!

Everyone was arriving, and before long, I heard the magical word that made everyone sit up and pay attention. The director calling out "Action!" into his mic; and a word to the wise, you had better not be in his shot. I've nearly been caught numerous times handing out Tylenol or taking a blood pressure on an extra and heard "Action! Roll 'em!" and quickly ducking down in the aisle or jumping behind a fence post, giving me shelter from the film's eager eye to catch everything in its view. After a scene was shot, the director would go into the tent housing the monitors where the scene was reviewed and the decision to reshoot or move onto the next scene was determined. A poster board on an easel with all the scenes scheduled to be completed for the day was also in the tent. It was a way of keeping everyone on schedule for the number of days allotted to make a movie.

"Medic! Medic! Medic!" my radio blasted through my headset. All morning the radio was so quiet I almost called security to do a radio check. Ha! That won't happen again! "Medic on 3, what's your location?"

"We're over by your station."

"Okay!" I answered, "I'll be right there!" I was met by the same group of men who started off my first day. The bedbug guys. "Hey, you are all looking better today! Show me." I motioned at them with a sweep of my finger, motioning them to lift their shirts so I could see how much progress was made overnight. Their skin, though not inflamed, looked angry. "Hmm. Did you all take a cool shower last night and rub on the steroid cream? Take your Tylenol and Motrin?" They all shook their heads affirmatively. "Did management move you into new rooms?" Three of the four said they had been moved. The fourth said his mattress was changed out and the carpet cleaned. "Well, keep up the treatment. We're making progress. I want to keep a close eye on you guys. Especially you," I said, pointing the guy whose ankles and midcalf were red and swollen from numerous bites. He was the boom operator, whose job was to get the microphone as close to the action as possible, without the equipment or its shadows showing up on camera. Because he was on his feet so much during filming, to reduce the swelling, I encouraged him to apply the cold pack I provided and elevate his legs as often as possible. Before the group went back to work, I instructed them to always apply the steroid cream in a downward stroke. I explained if the cream were applied incorrectly, it could get enmeshed in their hair follicles and cause a folliculitis or an inflammation of the hair follicle. It would be adding insult to injury. They all seemed to understand, so I sent them on their way with a plan to return to see me again first thing in the morning. I was filing my report, and the radio sounded off, demanding my assistance.

"Medic on 3!" I replied. "What's your location?"

Security responded, "By the arena. We have an injured extra."

I replied back into the headset, "I'm on my way!"

CHAPTER 24

To Seize or Not to Seize

I ARRIVED WITH MY backpack at the gate opening to the arena, and I found the stands already filled with the extras. *Getting started really early*, I thought. *Maybe we'll get out of here earlier tonight?* Ha! Fat chance! Now approaching the arena, I saw a woman on the ground in a sitting position. "Hi, I'm the medic. What's the problem here?"

"I think I had a seizure," she answered.

"You what? Why do you think you had a seizure?" I asked as I started assessing her from top to bottom automatically. She hadn't been incontinent (thank you) and didn't look like she'd fallen and hit her head. There were no complaints of nausea, emesis, and she was not having any tonic, chronic, seizure-like movements of any kind. *Okay*, I thought to myself, *I'll bite.*

"Why did you think you had a seizure?" I asked again

"Well, I was sitting up in the stands," she said, turning and pointing in the direction of the bleacher seats. "And the next thing I knew, I was sitting here on the ground!" I kept assessing her.

"Are you here with anyone?" I asked.

"No, I'm pretty sure I'm here all by myself," she answered.

"Okay..." I motioned to security. "Get her name from the roster and review her profile for an emergency contact number." I reached over and said, "Let me take your blood pressure. Seems okay," I said reassuringly after taking it. "Do you mind if I check your blood sugar? I will just take a small sample of blood. There we are. Now, your blood sugar level is ninety-eight. You had breakfast this morning?"

"Yeah, it was okay. They gave us cereal, toast, muffins, coffee, and juice."

"Sounds pretty good," I replied, thinking back about the ham, cheese, tomato, and mushroom omelet I had polished off just a short time ago. "Do you have a history of seizures?" I prodded gently.

"No, but when I realized I was sitting on the ground down here and couldn't remember how I got here, I was pretty sure I had a seizure."

"What kind of work do you usually do?"

"I'm a salesclerk, but I can't find any work right now. So I was really glad I was picked as an extra for this movie."

Hmm, I thought. "Okay. Here's the plan. Do you have a primary care physician? A doctor that you see all the time?"

"Uh-huh," she answered, looking quizzically at me. "Don't you want me in the movie today?"

"Yes, we do, but if you think you're having seizures, then you should have your doctor check you out. It's going to be very hot and humid again today, and what are we going to do if you think you might have another seizure while were filming? So we'll pay you for your time today. Then let the security officer take you back to base camp. How did you get here this morning?"

"I took a bus to the base camp this morning and then another bus brought us out here."

"Okay then. The security officer will transport you to base camp and will arrange for a cab to take you home for the remainder of the day. Do you have family that can help you get to the doctor's office?"

"Yes. I live with my sister, and she's at home right now."

"Good, good, good! So let's get going here. Feeling better?"

"Yes! Much!"

"Good. Officer, please escort this young lady back to base camp and arrange for a cab to take her home from there." I turned to the officer and said, "I'm filing a report to put in her record not to call her back as an extra. Perhaps she can apply and be an extra on another movie in town."

Most unfortunately, we do get many situations in production where an extra will seek medical attention. They will act like they are sick, and the production company will call in a doctor, rush them to the hospital, and foot the bill for all their medical expenses, but not if their vitals are stable, have no obvious bleeding, and are breathing without difficulty. They are excused, paid for the day, and never called back to work as an extra again. It seems harsh, but we're not a hospital. We're a production company trying to make a movie. There are so many people out of work in Detroit, which provides a huge pool of extras to pick from, so we can afford to ask an extra to leave. Their spot will be filled very quickly with someone who really wants to be an extra. Not a bad gig, actually, with three meals a day. They may not be fancy, but they are filling, and every extra is paid eighty dollars a day. The days can be very long, waiting and waiting for a scene to be filmed. Then when it is filmed, the director reviews it and will decide if they are going to reshoot the same scene at a different angle or with different lighting. In the meantime, the extras would sit for hours and hours on end waiting to hear the magic word—action!

CHAPTER 25

A Tattoo Could Save Your Life

I HEADED BACK TO my station but didn't get very far before I heard, "Medic, what's your location?"

"Heading back to my station," I replied. "Where do you want me to meet you?"

"Your station will be okay."

Mr. Blue Eyes was there waiting for me with another employee I had never met before, but I could tell he was a crew member.

"So who's first?" Blue Eyes said, pointing to the crew member I had never met before.

"How can I help you?"

He pulled up his shirtsleeve and showed me his arm. *Diabetic* was tattooed on the same arm as my diabetic from yesterday. I looked up at him. "Are you okay?"

"Yes," he said, smiling. "But I heard what happened and thought I should come over and introduce myself in case I got into trouble. Yesterday was tricky, but I got through the day and kept enough carbs on board so I wouldn't have an insulin reaction."

"Hey, thanks for letting me know," I said. "You're a gaffer, aren't you?"

"Yes."

"Well, would you fill this out for me?" I handed him a clipboard with a health history form attached. "I'll keep your information right here, so if I need to see you emergently, I can pull you up on my database. Where do you keep your insulin and glucometer?" He pulled around a fanny pack and showed me his supply of needles, alcohol wipes, insulin bottles, and a glucometer.

"You're amazing!" I told him. "I believe you and your buddy are the only two insulin-dependent diabetics on the crew." Note to self—ask the preproduction company before production starts if they know of anyone on the crew who were insulin-dependent diabetics. Most diabetics will be wearing a bracelet or amulet around their neck with the lifesaving information, like "I'm a diabetic" or "I have an allergy to sulfa or whatever." I usually spot those items right away from years of working in emergency rooms. But these tattoos were pure genius!

"Well, thanks again," I said as he was departing. "I think we're getting ready to film. I really appreciate you coming by."

Then I turned to Blue Eyes. "And what's going on with you?" He was already sitting down and had removed his shoes and socks.

"Please make them feel better again today."

"Okay," I said, smiling. "What helped yesterday?" As he went on with everything that had worked so well, I heard my radio.

"Medic! Medic! Medic, what's your location?"

I flipped the button to my headset and said, "I'm at my station. Do you need me somewhere?"

"No, we'll meet you there in a couple of minutes."

I turned back to Blue Eyes and finished up his feet and ankles and sent him on his way.

"Do me a favor and come back around two, if you can get away," I said to him. "I want to try something new."

"Okay," he said, walking away and passing up the security guard walking an extra up to the set.

"Hi, I'm the medic. How can I help you?" It turns out this wasn't an extra but someone who had brought a five-hundred-pound pig to the set to be used as a prop for a scene being filmed later in the day.

"Hi, I'm the set medic. Are you okay?"

"Yes," she said, smiling. "But I'm afraid I may have sprained my wrist trying to hang onto my pig this morning while we were getting him off the transport truck."

"Let me see." So it did look like a sprained wrist. I explained, "I'm not a doctor, and it is out of my scope of practice to diagnose, but I can make a guess. I am able do one of several things for you: I can wrap this with an ace, give you an icepack with some Tylenol and Motrin, and you can stay until the scene is completed today. Option 2, you could leave and let our property managers handle your pig while you go to urgent care and have your wrist x-rayed. Last option would be to take your pig home and go to the doctor's for treatment. You pick."

She had a warm smile and said, "I agree with all of your choices, and I choose choice number one. I can hang in there until the scene is done. I really don't want to leave my pig here, even though I know he'll get the best of care."

"Okay then. Let's get you fixed up!" We visited while I applied an Ace wrap and an ice bag to the injured wrist, then she left and returned to her pig. What a difference twenty-four hours can make. The heat index was rising, and the humidity just didn't know how to take a hint. It was going to be another brutal day with the weather. The calls kept coming in over the radio for the duration of the morning. I was just trying to figure out the best time to get to the ladies' room and change my clothes already sticking to me in odd places when one of the bullfighters appeared.

"Hey, Big John's in the pen!"

"Really!" I replied. "Then why are you here with me?"

He said, "Well, he's under control, but I thought you might want to know the cowboy who was gored yesterday is doing really well. Thanks for all of your help yesterday."

"Well, I really didn't do anything. I quipped back except provide him with a roll of cloth tape," I replied. "Did you guys know we have some really good tape that's been produced over the past few years, and it won't take your skin off when you remove it?"

"Yeah, but the cloth tape works really well!" he replied. "Were used to it, and he's doing great."

"Well," I replied, "I want an EMT to look at his wound. His skin was forcefully torn open, which is his first line of defense against getting an infection."

The rodeo clown finally agreed to allow the EMT to examine the cowboy's wound later in the afternoon, returning to his circle of friends.

CHAPTER 26

Feed a Pig an Apple, You Get Bacon

LUNCH WAS CALLED, and while I was looking for a table to sit in, a woman sitting at one of the tables called to me, "Sandy! Sandy! Come over here and join us!"

I looked over at her and said, "Hi. How do you know my name?"

She replied, "I worked with you on a movie with Clive Owen about eight months ago."

"Oh yeah! Gosh, I'm sorry. I was so distracted with the weather and all the calls. It's been a while. How are you?" She was one of the schoolteachers, and she shared a mutual interest in Hugh.

"Do you have any idea what I have been going through to try to meet him?" I said. He's always surrounded by his entourage. He's like Taylor Swift, only with guys! It's really difficult to get anywhere near him.

She laughed and said, "I know eventually we'll both get to meet him. What a cool guy; and he's so tall!"

I agreed with her right off. "Isn't he, though? Really surprised me. I had no idea. First time I saw him was yesterday just for a second, and I couldn't help but notice. What do you think? 6'4"? 6'5"?"

The end of lunch hour was nipping at our heels, and we both struggled to get up and out of our chairs. The ground was very wet, and the folding chairs we were in were sinking into the ground the longer we sat in them. Many of the chairs were sitting crooked by the end of lunch, and some of the crew had to crawl out on the sides of their chairs to come to a standing position. What a problem the rain had made!

How did we get through the second day? It was difficult but manageable. I had a few glimpses of Hugh again but not amounting to anything. I did spot him sitting in the director's tent looking at a scene on the monitor he had just completed. I could've walked in and just looked at him. But my radio started talking to me again.

One of the PAs had contacted me and explained, "We were filming a few extras on the graviton after lunch, and they started throwing up!" Duh! Stomach full of food, heat index of one hundred degrees, ridiculous humidity and riding the graviton, flying through the air at the speed of sound, right after eating a meal. Made me want to throw up just talking about it.

"Well, put them in the cooling tent," I said. "I'll be right there." I showed up to find four young men, in their early twenties, holding their heads and throwing up their lunches. Ew! I asked security to obtain their names and emergency contact information while I placed cold compresses across the back of their necks reducing the feeling of nausea instantly. It's the quickest cure for nausea. This group kept me busy for about thirty minutes, so I contacted security to call the EMTs away from their air-conditioned rig to give me a hand.

The director contacted me via one of the PAs and wanted to know how the extras were doing. I knew they were toast. No way would they be able to climb back into the ride and complete any of the scheduled scenes on the graviton. He quickly switched gears and moved onto a new scene scheduled for filming later in the afternoon that had the five-hundred-pound pig I met earlier in the day. This pig was the perfect example of a line Jim Gaffigan, one of my favorite standup comedians, said in one of his specials: "If you feed a pig an apple, he'll make bacon." This five-hundred-pound could fulfill his prophecy. I could only imagine how much bacon this pig was carrying around.

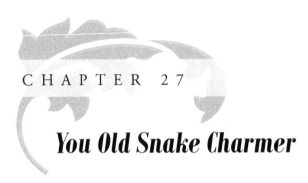

CHAPTER 27

You Old Snake Charmer

THE FIVE-HUNDRED-POUND PIG wasn't my first encounter with a pig. Years ago, when I was a homecare visiting nurse, I arrived at a patient's home in the early evening hours. The houses weren't located close together, not quite the country but not quite the city. The front door opened as I got out of my car, and five dogs on an enclosed porch came out jumping and barking. I reached in the backseat and pulled out of pair of high-top boots I kept just for visits like this. I grabbed my bag, and as I walked toward the house with the porch full of barking dogs, the owner poked his head around the corner and said, "Don't worry. They don't bite!" Shaking my head, I had to agree. Not one was snarling or baring their teeth. They just seemed happy and joyful to see me. "They're all rescues," the owner continued. "No one wanted any of them because there is something wrong with every one of them. See? This one's missing his hind leg. This one is blind in one eye, and his brother is missing an ear."

"Yes, I can see that!" I exclaimed. "I'm the visiting nurse. Where's the patient?"

"This way," he motioned through the door. As I walked in, I gasped. There, in a pen-like structure built from the floor up to the ceiling, with a locked door featuring a full-length window with a light shining in the pen. *What the...,* I thought. *This isn't a—oh yes, it was.* There was a huge snake lying on the floor, curled up. He looked comfortable for a snake. I noticed a birdcage next to the pen, but there is no bird in it.

The owner stepped up and said, "Yes, it's a snake, but don't worry. He can't get out."

I thought *Sure, he can't* as the dogs kept jumping up to my eye level all around me. *Then where is the bird?* I thought.

The owner of the house said, "Come this way. My wife's in the kitchen."

Thank God, I thought. *I want to get this visit over with and get out of here.* No one is going to believe this story! And no sooner had I thought that, I walked up to a three-hundred-pound potbelly pig lying on the floor between the living room and the kitchen, where my patient was waiting for me at the kitchen table.

"He won't hurt you, honey!" the patient said. "Just step over him. We all do!" I did just as she instructed and had a vision of the pig standing up and taking off with me riding him sidesaddle down the hallway. But Lady Luck was on my side tonight. I was able to see my patient and finish my visit with her in record time.

Now here I was, looking down the face of another pig, and I had a thought. *I don't think anyone back at the hospital is going to believe this story. Wish I could take a picture!* But even the mere thought of taking a picture on the set, in my mind, two security guards, materialized and walked up to me. For heaven's sake. What's so secretive on this movie even thinking about taking a picture silently in your head would get you thrown off the set? I was just going to have to give a mental image of this pig when I told the story to my friends and colleagues.

Just then, Blue Eyes showed up again. "So what's your new plan?" he asked.

"Come here and put these on!" I said, holding up a pair of tennis shoes that were just his size.

"Are you kidding me?" he asked.

"No, I'm not," I replied. "Try wearing these for just an hour and off-load the pressure sites on your feet. I'm hopeful we can break your cycle of pain. Humor me," I pleaded. "Just wear them for an hour. If it doesn't work, at least we tried! Look! I even put steel toes in them myself."

He put them on and walked away with no smile on his face and no twinkle in those baby blues. He just didn't have the confidence in me that I had in myself.

CHAPTER 28

Small-Town Charm

FILMING CONTINUED INTO the late afternoon hours, and I was treated with a view of Hugh doing a scene. I had the opportunity to just look at him. What was it that just drew you to him? He was seemingly oblivious to the magnetic draw he cast over everyone. Lighthearted, laughs easily, and could be wolverine man on command—what an actor; and lucky me that I got to watch him! The afternoon heat and humidity dragged on without mercy. The dinner hour was approaching, and my opportunity to change into dry clothes was all I could think about. Finally, the director yelled, "Cut! Break for dinner and be back here by 5:00."

No need to tell me twice. I was in the air-conditioned ladies' room taking off my clothes faster than a cheap prom dress. It felt good just standing naked in my tiny stall, letting the cool air surrounding me dry everything damp in its path. But in the interest of time, I gave into toweling myself dry while putting on dry clothes and hoping they would stay dry for the next five hours. Dinner was amazing. Everyone was settling into the rhythm and flow of the production of the movie.

Back to filming after dinner, I had given strict instructions for two of the extras kept over for the last few scenes of the night not to eat anything until the graviton scenes were completed. I could hardly keep my head on straight, watching the ride go round and round so fast. Really! Who pays money to ride this? Well, I'll tell you who! The minute the ride came to a stop during filming after lunch, Hugh broke out from the scene he was filming, ran over to the ride, and strapped himself in! Laughing and grinning, he yelled out, "Start this thing up!" He was wild! Everyone stopped what they were doing and watched him being spun out of control. I loved that about him. Hugh just embraced life and everything it had to offer. When the ride stopped, he unbuckled himself and was met with a round of applause from everyone. He returned to filming his scenes, and the martini shot, also referred to as the last shot of the day, was called. Before long, the day was over, and I was driving home feeling much more in control than my first day on set.

As the production of the film continued, I found out quickly how popular Hugh was. No matter where we filmed, there was always a group of loyal fans waiting to meet him. I would think out loud, "Get in line, people! I'm the set medic, and I still have only seen him from a distance." Yet he always made time after a day of filming to go out and sign autographs and take pictures with anyone who wanted an autograph. Once, we were filming in a small town and did not embrace the local police department for additional security because our security felt they could handle the locals. Wrong! It wasn't long before the locals were climbing up into the trailers and fingering everything we owned. Security quickly lost control of the unforgiving crowd that gathered. Nothing, and I mean nothing, was going to settle them down until they met Hugh. They kept our film crew and trailers hostages until Hugh sent out his assistant to gather them all in one area and promised he would be out to meet each and every one of them when he was done filming for the day. It took four hours, but the scenes Hugh was in were completed; and true to his word, he went out to the crowd, greeting and posing for pictures until everyone was satisfied. Who couldn't like this guy?

CHAPTER 29

Adiós

FILMING AT THE wheat field location was ending. The weather had been brutal, and the expression "If the heat doesn't get you, the humidity will" described our battle with the weather during the entire duration of filming at this location. No one was upset we were moving on. In retrospect, there wasn't anything anyone could have done that would have helped our time spent here be more bearable. A cooling tent was brought in, and we switched to night shoots to reduce our exposure to the heat and humidity. But then we had to deal with night time rainstorms in Michigan, which are never complete without the threat or appearance of a tornado. I bid a final farewell to the ambulance crew. Without them, I would have never gotten this gig. They had also turned out to be a godsend, helping me with the thousand or so extras appearing every day throughout the entire filming at this location site. I said goodbye to the cowboys and rodeo clown bullfighters. What a pleasure to meet them. I've always had respect for anyone who rides or stands in the path of a charging bull providing a safe exit for a cowboy thrown off its back. Watching them with a front-row seat renewed my respect for them. They have my vote if anyone wants to make bull riding, bullfighting, or rodeo clowning an Olympic sport.

CHAPTER 30

Oh, Henry!

OUR NEXT LOCATION was to the Highland Park Ford Plant, built in 1908 and opened in 1910, four and a half miles from downtown Detroit. The complex contained offices, factories, a power plant, and a foundry sitting on 120 acres of land, making it the largest manufacturing facility in the world at the time it was opened. It set the standard for how factories and production plants were built. I read this was the first automobile production facility in the world to implement the moving assembly line, and it could build a Model T in 93 minutes instead of 728. Since the time to build the Model T was so drastically reduced, Henry Ford lowered the price of the Model T from $700 dollars in 1910 to $350 in 1917, making the automobile affordable for most Americans. Nearly a century has passed, and now this facility is used by the Ford Motor Company to store documents for artifact storage for the Henry Ford Museum.

You could feel the presence of Henry Ford throughout the plant. Pictures of him hung everywhere, with pictures of the workers on the assembly line building the Model T. The building was literally drenched in history with a heavy, dank smell of engine oil and of a time long gone. The great news was that it was cool. No one seemed to mind that it was dirty and very old. The change in the climate was warmly welcomed, pun intended! Gone were the days of overexposure to the heat and humidity producing hypoglycemia, headaches, nausea, and dizziness. Now there was a new set of health issues to deal with: asthma flares, complaints of stinging eyes, and burning sore throats from the industrial air. We also filmed several fight scenes, and I was called to tend to bloody noses and bruised faces from misplaced punches.

CHAPTER 31

Magical Harry

THE CREW FILMED for several days at the Highland Park plant before we moved to downtown Detroit. After spending several days becoming reacquainted with the downtown area, I fell in love with Detroit all over again. The historical buildings were just magnificent. The men who built these buildings were true craftsmen, and it showed in every detail of their work. Beautifully carved stonework laid in place with such precision and pride. It's amazing what you can accomplish when you don't have cable TV to distract you. Our crew was preparing to film on the glorious Detroit riverfront, utilized for entertainment, just as it is today.

In 1926 my grandfather secured several tickets in a poker game to see the world famous magician, Harry Houdini, who was appearing on the Detroit riverfront. Grandpa drove my dad with a horse and buggy from Belleville about thirty-five miles away to see Harry Houdini pull off one of his most epic stunts on the Detroit Riverfront. Houdini, handcuffed and legs abound, jumped off the Belle Isle Bridge, into the Detroit River, and would prove to be one of the last performances this world-renowned illusionist and escape artist would ever perform, having developed peritonitis from a ruptured appendix. Houdini died one week later in room 401 at 1:26 PM at Grace Hospital in Detroit on October 31. He was fifty-two years old. His body was taken to the W.R. Hamilton and Company funeral home on Cass Avenue. There his body was embalmed and placed in a bronze coffin with a glass lid that Houdini wanted to use as a prop for his magic shows. The hospital where Harry died was torn down years ago, but the funeral home, now in disrepair, still stands on the corner of Cass and Alexandrine. Harry Houdini was then transported to New York City by railway. Over two thousand people attended his funeral.

CHAPTER 32

Mitzi

MOVING AWAY FROM the Riverfront, I found myself being directed by security to relocate my medic station in one of the oldest hotels in Detroit's history, the Pontchartrain Hotel, located across the street from an historical firehouse where we would film for several weeks.

Remember the tall willowy blonde who almost fired me on the first day of filming? Well, I read her bio just to wrap my head around who she was and her stake in the movie and realized what a highly respected person she was in the movie industry. It turned out she was the executive producer whose job was to ensure the film was completed on time, within budget, and to the agreed artistic and technical standards. I came to the quick realization how lucky I was I didn't lose my job the day she challenged me about using a cellphone on our first day of production. With just a look from her, security would have escorted me off the set, never to be heard from again in the movie industry. Now, by a strange twist of fate, I found myself rescuing a dog running as fast as her little legs could carry her right into the lobby of the Pontchartrain. She was an adorable Shih Tzu wearing a faux diamond collar and a name tag that read "Mitzi." Within a matter of a couple of minutes, I discovered the owner of this little cutie was the beautiful and mysterious blond executive producer running down the street with security guards in tow calling up Mitzi's name.

"Hmm," I said, looking at what I knew now was a real diamond collar. "I think you're in a lot of trouble right now with your mommy," I said to the puppy. I went to the door and flagged security yelling, "I have Mitzi!" The blond executive producer showed up breathless from running.

"You have my Mitzi?"

"Yes, actually she found me. She came running through the door just a few moments ago," I said, pointing to the grand front door of the hotel I had propped open to let fresh air in. I continued on, "My dog ran away on me once when I was taking a walk in the park. I was terrified I was never going to see him again!"

She was reaching for her dog and thanking me in the same breath. "Really. Thank you," she said sincerely.

"Really, it was nothing," I answered back. "I was just glad she ran in here and didn't get hit by a car. It's a pretty busy intersection just a block away."

We made small talk then she excused herself, walking away with Mitzi with a firm grasp. I have to say, after that morning, the executive producer no longer saw me as a threat to the integrity of the film. Whatever it was about me on the first day of production catching her attention and questioning my loyalty was now long forgotten. Still I was on a mission to figure out the big secret behind being guarded so carefully. Why wouldn't they let anyone take a picture? My curiosity in check, I kept a vigilant watch for anything out of the ordinary but cognizant of not looking too interested. I liked working as set medic on this movie and didn't want to unwittingly jeopardize my position ever again.

CHAPTER 33

Historical Detroit

THREE TIMES A day the crew would walk across the street to Cobo Hall for our catered meals. Cobo Hall, located at 1 Washington Boulevard is a convention center situated along Jefferson and Washington Avenues in downtown Detroit and named after Albert Cobo, mayor of Detroit from 1950 to 1957. The convention center was designed by Gino Rossetti and opened in 1960. At that time, it was the seventeenth largest convention center built in the United States. It certainly could not boast of the history the surrounding formidable buildings could brag about, but Cobo Hall had become the must stop venue for the biggest and wildest Rock and roll bands of the sixties and seventies, hosting Jimi Hendrix, the Rolling Stones, Black Sabbath, and Bruce Springsteen. Barack Obama spoke at Cobo early in his campaign trail but was the only sitting president since Eisenhower in 1960 to not attend an event at Cobo. One of the most historical events taking place at Cobo was Martin Luther King Jr.'s "I Have a Dream" speech. Although the speech was delivered at the 1963 March on Washington, making Martin Luther King Jr. a national icon, he had actually delivered this speech six weeks earlier in Detroit. It was released as a single on Motown records entitled "The Great March to Freedom."

Now the fire station we filmed at, as per information from HistoricDetroit.org, was a steel-frame, five-story Neoclassical building faced in brick and terra cotta (1929). Hans Gehrke, architect. The long-time home of Michigan's oldest fire department, the massive square headquarters building stood at a site occupied by fire department facilities continuously since about 1840 until the DFD moved out in 2013. The footprint of the building, located at the northeast corner of Washington Boulevard and West Larned Street, runs to the alley south of the Marquette Building and, on the building's east façade, to the building at 234 West Larned. The building is clad in dark red brick in a running bond pattern and trimmed in gray-buff terra cotta. A grey granite bulkhead rises about three feet in height. On the West Larned façade the building is divided into six bays, with the four central ones slightly projecting. These central bays contain the arched, terra-cotta-faced portals to four engine bays with deeply recessed double doors. To the engine bays' right shield bearing the DFD initials flanked by angels, one holding an axe, the other a pike. An identical surround in the same location at the façade's opposite end outlines a window. The pedestrian doors are surmounted by terra cotta crests marked "DFD" for Detroit Fire Department. In the entablature above the doors, is engraved the words "Fire Headquarters." The four fire engine doors are outlined by terra-cotta-trimmed arches displaying rope moldings, detailed lintels, and keystones. A rosette in a circle decorates each spandrel. The first level is a story and-a-half tall to accommodate the fire trucks. A terra-cotta belt course separates the first level from the second story above. The banks of windows above are set in closely spaced pairs above the engine bays and singly at the ends. The original wooden double-hung windows are still in place, many containing air conditioning units. Between the second and third stories appears another broad terracotta band containing a dentilled cornice. The walls above are demarcated into bays by broad and shallow piers supporting a tall terra-cotta entablature with dentilled cornice topped by anthemion cresting. Metal spandrel panels separate the third and fourth-story and fourth and fifth-story windows in the center four bays. The Washington Boulevard façade has much of the same detailing, but there were some differences. There were three engine bays in the center with a large window at either end in the street level of the projecting center section of the façade and an entrance—pedestrian at the right and roll down vehicular at the left—at either slightly recessed end of the façade. Above the north and south doors are cartouches containing firefighter horns and hats.

The history of these buildings just took my breath away!

CHAPTER 34

Wait, What? Who?

THE FOOD PROVIDED by catering was just fantastic. I was enjoying my renewed friendship with the set teacher I had reconnected with. We usually met up for lunch every day. One day, at lunch, I was going on about an extra I had treated just prior to the break when I noticed, while I was talking to her, that she was looking right over my shoulder, not even appearing to be listening to me. I stopped talking, a bit annoyed, taking her chin in my hand saying, "For heaven's sake! What is wrong with you?"

She reached over without shifting her eyes and took my chin in her hand, turning my head, so I was looking over my shoulder. There, walking directly toward our table was Hugh Jackman. He was headed right for our table. As he passed other crew members already seated at other tables, they stopped talking and just stared at him. People literally just stopped what they were doing and stared at him, and I was no different. No matter how many times I saw him in a day, and I was seeing him every day, several times a day, I always stopped what I was doing and just watched him. What was it about Hugh that had this kind of effect on people? Lucky guy. But here I was, frozen in place. I was riveted. It was like a mirage walking toward us. Closer and closer he came. I forgot how to talk. He was carrying a lunch tray. Was he going to sit down and have his lunch with us? What would we talk about? How long would he stay? What if my radio went off and demanded I leave and render aid to someone in distress? My mind was already made up; they would have to wait! I wasn't getting up and leaving this table for anyone! He kept sauntering toward our table. Now, up close, he didn't look as tall as he did from a distance. I thought, *It must have been the kerchief he was wearing around his neck the first time I caught a glimpse of him.* And his chest and shoulders weren't as broad and beefy-looking as they were in the movies. He just looked… wrong! He stopped at our table and looked down at me and said "G'day!"

I finally found my voice and said, "You're not Hugh Jackman!"

"I never said I was!" the gentleman countered back. "Hi!" he said, reaching out and shaking my hand. "My name is Taris. I'm Hugh's body double."

I kept staring at him and was physically trying to wrap my head around the fact that just a minute ago, I was thinking, as did many of the crew, that Hugh Jackman was going to sit down and have lunch with us. As if! What was I thinking? Obviously, I wasn't, or I would have never thought it to begin with. I finally pulled myself together and said, "Glad to meet you?"

He laughed and said, "You sound so disappointed. I'm sorry. I get that a lot." He was a funny guy with a great sense of humor. It made me pause to think of all the times I had seen Hugh on the set, or was it him?

"Well, I can't say I've seen you around before, Taris. How could I have missed you?"

"Well, I've been Hugh's body double for a while. A lot of people say, when they see us together, they think we're brothers. They use me to set the stage for Hugh before a scene is shot. Where to stand, the lighting, camera angles, anything that needs to be addressed before Hugh gets in front of the camera. I've traveled all over the world with him."

"Well, you are one lucky guy, aren't you, Mr. Taris?" I said, smiling back at him. "Now, what can I do for you? I doubt you just wanted to join us for lunch."

"Two lovely ladies like yourselves?" He went on, "I heard you were the set medic, and I have a favor to ask of you."

"Well, let's hear it then, but I'll only help you under the condition you set up a private audience for my friend and I with Hugh." He thought it was a fair exchange and finished having his lunch with us. Taris was a blast, and he joined us for lunch many times after my first mistaken-identity meeting! But now I was paying attention to Hugh, or who I thought was Hugh, when I saw him on the set. I actually got very good at telling the two of them apart. Hugh was much taller!

CHAPTER 35

Ouch!

"**M**EDIC! MEDIC! MEDIC, what's your location?" My radio barked at me. "Medic on 3, what's your location?"

"I'm at Cobo Hall just finishing up lunch. Where is your emergency?"

"We are at the catering truck just outside the back door of the lunch hall."

"I'll be there in a minute. Bye, guys. I have to go," I said, grabbing my backpack and running off. I ran out the back doors to the loading dock and found the owner of the catering company sitting on the edge of his truck holding his hand and rocking back and forth. There wasn't any blood I could see, thank God, but what I did see made me cringe. Apparently, he had lost his footing exiting backwards off the catering truck and fell hitting his face on the door, landing with his full weight on his hand on the edge of the truck. He tore off the thumbnail on his right hand, trying to stop his fall.

"Well, I know you're not going to let me touch that hand, sir. Security, please get us this young man a transport van and have him transported to the Detroit Receiving Hospital ER. I don't have the pain medication you need to get the situation under control. Trust me, sir. This is the best plan. Your crew will cover for you while you're gone," I reassured him. "Lunch is over, and it was delicious," I said, trying to lift his spirits.

He smiled back, but it was painful to even exert that much energy. The van showed up, and he was on his way. I was filling out the accident report and my radio went off again.

"Medic! Medic! Medic, what's your location?"

"Medic on 3. Back at my station. Where do you need me?"

I ran across the street to the alley behind the fire station. One of the cameramen was sitting on the ground, rubbing a big knot forming on the back of his head, and it was bleeding "What did you do?" I asked.

"Oh, the stupid rig," he said, pointing to the cherry picker in the alley. "I was getting on it, and someone yelled at me while I was getting on. I got up too fast, and I hit the rail. Hard."

"Yes, you did." I confirmed looking at his bleeding scalp. "All right. You're going to live. Let me clean this up and see if you need any stitches." He started to protest, and I held up my hand and said, "Don't even say it. At the very least, I'm going to clean the blood away so I can see what I'm dealing with here. Sit still. I'm not sending you home." I cleaned the wound up but could tell that the gash he sustained needed a few stitches. If it were smaller, I could have just put some Steri-Strips, some bacterial ointment, and a dressing on, but not this time. I had checked his records, and his last tetanus shot was just a year ago, so he was off the hook for needing a tetanus shot, but I was very firm in telling him he was going to the ER to get stitched up. He fussed but resigned his fate to the inevitable.

"Cripes," he sputtered. "If it's not one thing, it's been another on this movie."

I answered back, "You're preaching to the choir, mate!" A transport van showed up and took him on his way to the ER. I said, "You know, I just sent the owner of the catering company there. If you're lucky, you two might get to share the bay area."

He laughed and said, "Very funny! I'll see you later." He waved and was gone.

I was cleaning up the area and restocking my dressing tray when the head PA said, "You're out of here! We're done filming for the day, and all the trucks and gear are secured. Have a great three-day weekend! You deserve it!"

"What?" I said.

"I said have a great three-day weekend. We have Monday off because of the holiday." I had completely forgotten about the holiday. I had been so busy I actually had forgotten about it. What a treat! Three days off in a row. I was almost giddy. I slept in on Saturday, washed clothes, mowed the lawn, played with the dogs, went to the farmer's market, and did some grocery shopping. I treated myself to breakfast. I had become so spoiled eating on the set three times a day and munching on goodies Crafty services put out all day. I was literally shocked when I got my breakfast bill. This costs how much? What a shock to see what the rest of the world was paying to eat out. I rested the entire weekend and felt like a new person on my return to work.

CHAPTER 36

A Quiet Tuesday

THE CREW RETURNED to work on a beautiful Tuesday morning. The sun was rising over the city, casting a warm glow over the towering historic buildings. The historical fire station looked so welcoming with its antique red bricks. Many stories were enfolded in those walls, waiting for someone to come by and ask them to tell what they had seen and heard over the last century. The crew was just starting to move around. Our call sheet listed call time at 8:00 AM. Everyone was exchanging morning greetings, drinking coffee, and eating breakfast burritos from the catering truck, just a restful, quiet morning.

I was busy setting up my medic station for the day, popping open my jump kit and plastic totes brimming with Ziploc bags full of a treasure trove of medical supplies. A tremendous array of treatment paraphernalia, I had organized and made all the medical supplies user-friendly for any crew member to help themselves to anything they might need if I was busy elsewhere on the set. It was just blissfully quiet; I could even hear a bird singing! Then *boom!* Out of nowhere, visible to anyone on the set, an urgent call came over my radio.

"Medic! Medic! Medic, give us your location!" I jumped out of my chair, putting on my gloves on at the same time running through the lobby of the hotel and out onto the street. I looked up and down the street for the source of the call. "Medic! Medic, what's your location?

"Medic on 3. I'm in the middle of the street across from the fire station. Identify yourself. Where is your emergency?" Almost instantly it appeared at the end of the street, west of the set. A Detroit police car screeched to a halt at the end of the street, with a police officer jumping out of the car at the same time. The urgent look in his eyes made me glad I had grabbed my medic bag on my way out of the hotel just moments earlier.

He yelled at me, "Medic? Medic? Are you the medic?"

"Yes, where's your emergency?"

"It's too far to walk!" he yelled back.

"Hop in, and I'll drive you there." My first thought was, *Too far to walk?* I didn't know what the emergency was, but I didn't think I would be walking toward it when I finally arrived. I was expecting to be more like running! Now I was the one yelling at him "Go! Go! Go!" The officer whipped in and out of traffic, careening through traffic lights and stop signs. They were just in our path. I didn't have enough time to ask what happened when, all of a sudden, a scene right out of *M*A*S*H* was unfolding right in front of me.

"Oh my god! Oh my god!" I said out loud and thought simultaneously, *I had not brought along enough ice bags.*

The source? A transport bus bringing twelve to fifteen extras to the set for the first scenes of the day had somehow overcorrected making a turn, rolling several times, landing on its wheels. None of the extras had been wearing a seat belt. The roof of the van was crumpled like an accordion, with debris sticking up at odd angles, exposing the inside of the bus to the clear blue sky above. Windows were broken, and a steady stream of steam was curling out from under the hood.

I looked at the officer and asked, "Have you called for emergency backup?"

"Yes." He nodded. "The ETA is anywhere from fifteen minutes to two hours for an ambulance to arrive."

"What? Get back on the radio and call them again. Tell them to get here *now*. We have multiple catastrophic injuries. It looks like a battlefield!" Even fifteen minutes was going to be an eternity. I grabbed my bag and ran around to the front of the bus where screams and cries for help were coming from every direction.

"Help me, please! Help me!" Hands were reaching out and grabbing me for immediate assistance.

I quickly scanned the field where about fifteen extras were sitting on the ground with everything, from broken knees, ankles to legs. It was hard to identify the exact injuries, but everyone was breathing, and no one appeared to be bleeding and needing immediate intervention. I ran back to the side of the bus and found a young girl in her twenties lying on the steps half in and out of the bus. I felt her carotid. She was conscious with a very rapid heart rate.

"Are you breathing okay?" I asked. She nodded her head up and down very slowly. "Can you move your legs and arms?" Again, she nodded yes. I reached in my bag and pulled out a cervical collar and gently placed it around her neck. "I'm going to get help. Stay right here." She was disturbingly quiet. I stepped over her and got onto the bus.

The driver was still seated and awake. I felt for his pulse. "Sir, do you hear me? Are you okay? Sir! Can you hear me?" He nodded his head. His respirations were around twenty-four and had a weak but palpable pulse. My best guess was, he hit his chest against the steering wheel on impact, probably sustaining a cardiac contusion, a bruise to the heart, which would be sorted out in the ER. Right now, I just wanted to make sure he kept a patent airway. I couldn't visualize any bleeding anywhere on him, so I turned and headed for the slumped-over figure in the back of the bus.

"Sir? Sir? Are you okay?" Oh my god, it was one of our PAs! I recognized him right away. He lifted his head and threw up immediately. I pulled out an ice bag and put it up against the knot on his forehead. "Help is on the way! Stay put!" I turned to the security officer who followed me onto the bus.

"Get on your radio. Request a survival flight crew from the closest hospital that has one. I have a critically injured person needing immediate transport." Pointing out the window, I said to the police officer, "See the open field? When you call the chopper, advise them we have an area big enough for them to land. Have the other officers secure the landing site right now! As soon as you call for the chopper, it will be arriving before you know it! Go. Now!" He ran off the bus yelling into his radio. I exited the front of the bus and turned to another police officer waiting for me. I said to the young girl on the steps, "We're going to move you now, okay?"

The officer and I gently picked her up and laid her down on the grass not far from the opening of the bus. The minute we laid her flat on her back, she became agitated, restless, diaphoretic, and short of breath. *What had I missed?* I thought frantically. I turned her onto her side and lifted her blouse. I spotted the culprit right away. On the lower side of her chest was an opening no bigger than a dime with bloody drainage and bubbles—a telltale sign of a pneumothorax, a traumatic opening into the lining of the wall of the chest cavity during the collision, allowing air in and out of her lungs with every breath she took.

Lying on her side against the wound, she had put enough pressure against the opening, closing the wound enough so air was not entering and exiting through the site. It would have never lasted. Within a short amount of time, she would have gone into respiratory distress whether she continued to lie on her side or during the move, putting her flat on her back. She had a "sucking" chest wound. I had to act quickly. I pulled out a piece of Vaseline gauze and held it up against the open wound—a temporary fix that would only last moments. Where was the chopper? The young girl kept looking at me with a look of dread in her eyes.

"Stay with me, stay with me!" I kept urging her keeping my hand over the wound in her chest. "Help is almost here" Where is that survival flight chopper? *Please get here now!* I prayed. This young girl needed lifesaving interventions immediately. Then my prayers were answered.

No sooner had I uttered the thought in my head about where was the chopper than I heard it approaching. I looked over my shoulder and could see trees, bushes, dirt, everything turning into a whirling debris as the chopper made its descent. The sound of the blades was deafening. The extras' cries for help were silenced. Finally, the chopper was on the ground. The door flew open, and not two, but three medical personnel jumped off. I couldn't believe my eyes! Security was ushering them toward me. I waved with my one free arm. In a moment, they were standing next to me. I could tell by their badges two were RNs, and the other was a flight surgeon. Oh my god! What were the chances of getting a flight surgeon? I didn't care! I needed every one of those professional hands and their lifesaving equipment.

"I'm sure she has a pneumothorax!" I yelled. "She's in acute respiratory distress and is my most critical patient I'm aware of. The driver needs help next," I said, motioning with my head. "I believe he has a cardiac contusion. He hit the steering wheel really hard on impact. He's conscious, has a pulse, and respirations are unlabored."

Their treatment bags opened succinctly while I heard the sound of ambulances filling the air. *Oh sure, now they show up!* I thought to myself. Five ambulances came screeching to a halt. Paramedics and medics were jumping out of their rigs with their treatment packs. I turned my attention back to my patient with the pneumothorax.

The RNs were placing two large bore needles in each arm and started to administer IV fluids and medications, relieving the pain and anxiety this poor girl had been enduring for what probably seemed like an eternity to her. The IV medications put her into an unconscious state. The doctor had opened the box containing the equipment to intubate her, which meant he would be placing an ET, or endotracheal tube, into her lungs to breathe for her. Beautifully trained hands were taking the curved steel blade and putting it down her throat. With the tube in place, the nurse auscultated to make certain both lungs were getting air supply bilaterally before inflating the balloon and taping the ET in place. Next, the nurse opened a kit containing a chest tube. The doctor was going to place the tube right here, in the middle of the field, next to this pile of mangled steel into her lung with the pneumothorax. The second nurse opened another bag that contained a Pleur-Evac. This was a container that collected the bloody pleural fluid, which was collecting in the cavity of the lung. One nurse took over, "bagging" the patient with the Ambu bag, when the doctor turned his attention to inserting the chest tube.

She continued to bag while the doctor wordlessly inserted the chest tube and stitched it into place before attaching the Pleur-Evac. Then the doctor opened the clamp of the Pleur-Evac, and bloody drainage came out immediately through the chest tube. The Pleur-Evac connections to the chest tube were taped into place. The RN kept bagging the ET tube with an Ambu bag to assure the patient continued to get the oxygen needed

Once the doctor and the nurses felt the patient was safe for transport to the hospital and the waiting ICU team, the doctor said, "Okay, let's go!" A gurney appeared out of nowhere, and the young girl was lifted ever so gently by the doctor, nurses, a security guard, and myself. We transferred her into the waiting helicopter. Then, as if on silent command, the pilot started the chopper up. Within moments the chopper blades were in motion, going faster and faster! The chopper took off rising higher and higher! Dirt leaves, tree branches, anything in the path of the chopper was flying in every direction on the ground. I covered my face with my blood-covered hands and watched the helicopter hover for just a moment overhead. Then it was gone.

CHAPTER 37

A Battlefield

"MEDIC, MEDIC? EXCUSE me, are you the medic?"
"What?" I said, looking over in the direction of the voice talking to me. "I'm so sorry," I said, collecting my thoughts and regrouping. I just couldn't seem to move. My feet seemed to be imbedded in concrete. "Yes, I'm the medic," I managed to get out. "How can I help you? Are you okay?"

"Not really." He was holding his left arm up with his right hand supporting it. I changed my gloves and kept looking at him.

When I finally had a new set of gloves on, I said gently, "Here, let's sit down. Let me see this." I reached over and retrieved my backpack. When he was seated on a piece of concrete nearby, I very slowly removed his hand and the shirt he was holding over his arm. *Oh god,* I thought when I looked at the injury. He was another one of the extras that was injured in the accident.

"Let's get you some help right away." I could feel a pulse, but for how long, it was yet to be determined. "You must be in tremendous pain," I said, eyeing him up and down. "How have you managed to stay so quiet? You know you probably have several broken bones here. Did you put your arm out to protect yourself when the van rolled?" He shook his head up and down, and his eyes were beginning to well up with tears.

"Medic, Medic!" I motioned over to the paramedic triaging the injured. "This young man needs transport to the trauma center as soon as possible." The medic quickly looked at the injury. He picked his head up and looked at me.

"Yeah, let's transport him next. Come on, buddy." He was on his radio talking to the doctor at the trauma center triaging his calls. "This is Medic One to Base One. I have a fractured arm. Male, early twenties. We'll be transporting in the next ten minutes."

"Yes, sir," he answered while continuing to listen to the squeaking from his radio. He led the young man away, and I walked out onto the battlefield.

There were five ambulances onsite triaging and transporting two to three injured extras at a time. There were a lot with head and eye trauma. Two had a broken knee. When the roof crashed in on impact, debris went flying everywhere. I looked back into the bus and was relieved to see that the driver was finally gone. I turned to the medic next to me. "Did you treat the driver?"

"He was being so stubborn and kept insisting everyone else first," he answered.

"I know."

"I… I… I just couldn't get him to move out of that driver's seat. Doesn't matter. I wouldn't have been able to treat him then anyways. I had my hands full with the young girl in respiratory distress."

"Well, I'm just glad you finally got to him."

"Yeah, he was one of the first ones we transported out of here. Hey, really nice work on that pneumothorax. Pretty crazy, huh?"

"You know it. I was really scared I was going to lose her there for a minute. I was glad the survival flight showed up when they did. I'll have to call the trauma center when I get back and see how she's doing."

Finally, the last extra was loaded into the last remaining ambulance, and the tow truck was gone with the mangled van. The field was covered in all kinds of debris. Bloody four-by-fours, drain sponges, abdominal pads, syringe wrappers, exam gloves; there just wasn't any time for anyone to dispose of anything except to just throw it on the ground. I picked up my radio and called security on 10. "This is the

Medic on 3. I need a ride back to the set and send help to pick all the medical debris up off this field." I looked around one more time. I grabbed my backpack and turned to get into the transport van approaching to pick me up. When I got in, even though it was only going to be a five-minute ride, I took the time to put my seat belt on.

CHAPTER 38

My, What Big Feet You Have!

I WAS QUIET DURING the drive back to the set, feeling totally beaten up as I dragged myself over to the medic station and threw my backpack on the table. I stared at it for a minute then started to review all the contents and replaced everything I had used. I had to be ready for whatever might happen next. I walked across the street to the fire station. The crew was setting up the next scene. Adjustments had to be made to the schedule to film alternate scenes that were meant to be filmed this morning. I watched everyone scurrying around, preparing the set. I turned away and leaned against the fire station. The ancient red bricks warmed to the touch from the sun bearing down on them in the middle of the day. I ached everywhere, and the heat from the bricks felt like I was putting a gigantic heating pad up against me. I was in heaven. I became so absorbed in the moment of the heat from the building bringing such kind relief to my entire body and my radio remaining quiet. I just put my head down, closed my eyes, and relaxed.

Taris walked up and put his arm around my shoulder.

"That was really something you did out there this morning." His voice was so pleasant and calm. I could listen to him all day.

"Thanks, but I was just doing my job. I'm really very lucky everything turned out the way it did. It could have been a lot worse, but I think everyone is going to be okay," I said.

"Well, all the same." Taris went on, "I couldn't have done what you did."

"Oh," I replied, "you would be surprised what you can do when there's an emergency like this, Taris. The adrenaline just takes over, and you start doing whatever needs to be done." I kept looking down, still absorbing the heat from the bricks soothing my aching back and staring down at the ground, "Jeez, Taris! I had no idea your feet were so big!" The answer surprised me.

"Well, if they belonged to Taris, they wouldn't be now, would they? Seeing as how he wears a nine, and I'm an eleven." I looked up slowly at the face staring down at me. Oh my god, it was Hugh Jackman. He was so tall. The smile on his face was incredibly sweet, and I just stood there unable to say anything.

"Thought I was Taris, eh? Well, he's a great stunt double, but I didn't think the only way you could tell us apart was by the size of our feet!"

A PA appeared and said, "Mr. Jackman, we're ready for you now."

Hugh took his finger and just barely touched the end of my chin. "Gotta go! G'day!" And he walked away. Just like that.

CHAPTER 39

Buggers and Flowers?

"MEDIC, MEDIC, MEDIC!" my radio demanded. I kept staring at the back of Hugh's head disappearing into the fire station. Nothing on the face of the earth could wipe the smile off of my face. I finally answered my radio, "I'm in front of the fire station with Hugh Jackman."

The voice on the radio replied, "Well, do you think you could tear yourself away long enough from Mr. Jackman and come to the rooftop of the fire station? We have a slip and fall needing your attention." After the morning I had, a slip and fall sounded like a piece of cake. I made my way up the winding and narrow one-hundred-year-old-plus stairwell opening onto a rooftop bursting with every flower imaginable.

The flowers were in pots on the floor, next to patio chairs, hanging from shepherd's hooks, mounted in large pots in any space available. There were pastel blossoms of impatiens, petunias, black-eyed Susans, corn flowers, sunflowers, zinnias, marigolds, daisies, peonies, hydrangeas, star gaze lilies, salvia, freesia, roses, bellflowers, just a bountiful array of every flower one could imagine. This beautiful secret garden was just moments away from the hustle and bustle of the traffic flow below and on the rooftop of a fire station! Pure genius. This had to be the work of a master gardener with whom I held, without ever meeting, the highest respect. I had no luck at all trying to grow anything. My dearest friends knew never to buy me a plant because they knew within a week, in spite of my best attempts, the plant would be dead. My only skill to date was saving lives, and I was good at it. If you were going to have any skill at all, saving lives was a good one to have. However, whenever the opportunity presented itself, and I was lucky enough to come upon a garden of flowers like this one, I took a picture of it and put it in my logbook to look back on when my day was not going so well. It always brought back a peaceful and warm memory.

Another local Detroit spot to find an eclectic collection of flowers is one mile northeast of downtown Detroit, the Eastern Market, originally called the Farmer's Market, which opened in 1841 at Cadillac Square in the downtown area. In the beginning, the market was devoted to sales of hay and wood, but in 1891, it evolved into sales sheds that were built. The market was moved from Cadillac Square to its present location and renamed the Eastern Market, which is the largest open-air flowerbed market and the largest historic public market district in the United States. More than 150 food and specialty businesses are located within the market district, selling all types of goods including produce, meat, spices, jams, flowers, and poultry. The Eastern Market Historic District was added to the National Registry of Historic Places in 1978. Located in Detroit, Michigan, it had 150 years of rich history defining Detroit.

Now I was standing in the doorway of the entrance to the flower garden and could see the injured crew member lying just to the left of the doorway, clutching his left foot. I recognized him as one of our cameramen. He had run downstairs to pick up something he had forgotten and was coming back through the door and tripped over a tract being laid for one of the scenes.

"Bugger! Bugger! Bugger! So stupid. How could I be so stupid?" he kept saying.

I took one look at the angry, swelling, tender-to-the-touch blue ankle and said, "Hi, I'm Sandy, your set medic. Tripped, eh?" I gently reached for the injured ankle. "I know that hurts. I have help on the way. You'll have to go to the local ER and get this x-rayed, but it does look broken. Can you bend or move it at all?" Unfortunately, he could not.

"I'm going to wrap this," I said, securing an ace wrap around the foot and ankle. "It's going to help with the pain and swelling, but not a lot." I took a set of vitals while waiting for security to arrive and secured an ice bag for the swelling ankle. It was going to be an ordeal getting him back down the narrow staircase.

Security arrived, and I basically just got out of the way while they started to maneuver him down the stairwell. An order was put out by radio that no unnecessary crew was allowed up on the roof until the scene being shot was completed, helping to avoid any additional injuries waiting to happen with an excess number of staff lingering around and leaving things in harm's way in such a small and confined area. The day marched on, and calls for the medic were nonemergency. Mostly headaches, a scraped knee, and removing a splinter were all I had to deal with. The PA radioed me later in the evening and said the last truck is closed up. It's time to go home. Hallelujah! You didn't have to tell me twice. I was gone and not in any big hurry to return.

CHAPTER 40

Finally, the First Meeting

I HAVE BEEN ON a movie set with and without extras. Without extras is infinitely better. I still had my fair share of radio calls from the crew, but things really got back to normal when it was two hundred crew members and myself. No drama, no tragedies.

We had moved on to another location in Michigan, and I was busy setting up my work station, visiting with a few of the crew, chatting and waiting for filming to begin. Then I saw him, just a short distance away, outside the building we would be filming in for the rest of the day—Hugh, sitting in his director's chair, reading the script, and looking like he was memorizing his lines for the day. There was no one anywhere near him for a country mile. No one, not a director, producer, PA, makeup, wardrobe, family, body double, no one. I excused myself from the crew visiting with me and started to approach where he was sitting. *Anytime*, I thought to myself. *Anytime now someone is going to walk up and steal any time I could have with him away from me.*

Closer I approached him. Still no one. Hugh kept looking down and continued to read the script. I kept quietly approaching, thinking if I stepped on a twig, it would signal security to show up and intervene. But still, no one! Hmm, I hesitated for a second. I was maybe five feet away from him, and still he was able to draw me in like a magnet. Such charisma. Lucky guy. I decided to continue walking forward. What did I have to lose? I waited literally weeks to even get this close to him. Then there I was, standing right in front of him. I totally froze. I just stood there and just looked at him. After a moment, maybe two, Hugh looked up at me and smiled. I just melted.

Somehow, something inside of me spoke and said, "Hi, Mr. Jackman. I know we've never really been introduced to each other," I just kept blabbing on. "It wasn't for lack of trying! You have such an entourage of people around you all the time. I could never get close enough." He just sat there and continued to smile at me. "I'm Sandy, the set medic. But you know that already. You really took me for a surprise that day you came up to me after the really big accident. Well, I… I… I don't want to keep you from reading your script. Doubt you'll ever need anything from me, but you never know!" I stuttered on. I was going to turn and walk away searching for anything hard to hit my head on—a doorframe, camera, cherry picker. Really? How could I not find anything better to say? I'm glad I dazzled him with my clinical skills because talking to him was clearly not my forte. I heard him speak as I was turning away.

"Good to finally meet you too. I've seen you racing around here like a crazy lady. Especially on the first day of filming."

"You saw that?" I replied, thinking back with only a vision of rain-drenched clothes, hair sticking to my face, and glasses so totally fogged over I couldn't see where I was going. "Oh, that was the worst day I have ever spent on a movie set. You only saw a small portion of it. I thought it was never going to end. Well, the worse day next to the bus-rolling-over accident. I really appreciated everything you said that day. I have to say, you and Taris really do sound alike. I never would have looked up if I hadn't noticed the size of your feet. Some girls look at smiles, but I look at feet. Go figure!" He had the biggest and warmest smile. I could have kept talking forever.

Just then, a PA walked up and said, "Mr. Jackman, we're ready for you now."

He got up and turned to me and said "G'day" and walked away. I don't know why, but after finally meeting, my encounters with him were really pleasant and comfortable. I literally started bumping into him every day after that. No time to chat, but I would give a quick wave or say "Morning. Need anything?" or "Have a good day." All the memories of the terrible days I had endured before actually getting to meet him were totally forgotten with just one of his smiles. Lucky set medic!

CHAPTER 41

Honeybees and Mustard

BEES, HUNDREDS AND hundreds of bees, were everywhere at our next location site. They weren't just the garden variety of bees, but hybrid wasps. I grew up on a farm and never encountered bees as big as these were. The stings they were leaving behind on anyone who got into their path were all-consuming. We had moved to the country about an hour's drive from Detroit and were filming at an old farmhouse with numerous outlying buildings filled with wasp nests. We were so isolated. I ensured I had plenty of extra supplies packed before we hit the road, but I never expected wasps. Honestly, you have to be ready for anything when you're on location. Anything. I kept busy most of the afternoon, removing stingers and applying cold compresses to the bitten sites swelling up at record speed. Watching the beestings swell up triggered a childhood memory when I was about five or six.

I was playing with my sisters under an apple tree in the orchard and, without any warning, I remember getting intense pain in the back of my neck. My screams brought my mother flying out of the house, looking for which one of her ten kids was in distress. When she saw me clutching at my neck and just continuing to scream, she knew what had happened. I had been bitten by wasps; fifteen to twenty bites were her memory of the incident. She quickly took me into the house and put a cold cloth on the bites. I felt small relief, enough to calm me down for a second or two, long enough for her to make a paste out of baking soda and water. She put the soothing mixture over the bites on my neck, and in just moments, I had such relief. Mom and I didn't know it at the time, but bee venom has formic acid, and the baking soda, which had bicarbonate, an alkali, neutralized the effect of the bee venom. Mom never did figure out why it worked. She just knew it did. We not only had wasp bites to contend with but also bites from honeybees. My dad had beehives on another part of the farm, and if you got too close to his hives, the honeybees would let you know it! All ten of my siblings at one time or another endured the sting from a honeybee. The cure for a bite from this bee was easy—just apply honey! Not only was it soothing, it had a natural antibacterial ingredient that protected the body part bitten by from infection.

I didn't have time to mix up a baking soda paste for these wasp bites. Hmm, I needed to use something else. I remembered reading about a herb the Egyptians used centuries ago for bee and insect bites when I was in nursing school. I got online and looked up ancient herbal remedies. I found the answer in a short amount of time and only had to go to catering to get what I needed, a big jar of mustard. Of course, the ancient Egyptians didn't have Grey Poupon at their beck and call, but they did have mustard seeds, which are rich in selenium, a wonderful anti-inflammatory agent. Applying mustard directly to the area of the wasp bite now was my first line of treatment against the attack of these noble warrior wasps. I continued to treat the beestings with great success throughout the day until one of the crew members had an allergic reaction. It was bound to happen with as many of the crew being bitten.

I had prepared for hours in anticipation of this very thing happening. The crew member, the production manager, who, within moments of being bitten, felt his lips and face began to swell, with a feeling of dread overwhelming him. I had received the call, "Medic! Medic! Medic! We need you *stat* on the set." I was there in a moment, carrying a syringe of epinephrine in my hand. I knew in my gut what the call was going to be about. Good thing I came prepared! The production manager's face was swelling up like a balloon, and his voice was getting very raspy.

"I'm having trouble breathing!" He didn't have to say it. I could see it in his eyes, the look of impending doom. His immune system was overreacting to the allergen being released by the beesting. I showed him the syringe that read "Epinephrine." He shook his head affirmatively, and I gave him the injection into the lateral thigh (vastus lateralis muscle).

Turning to security, I said, "Call an ambulance. Tell them we have a crew member having an anaphylactic reaction to a beesting." I turned back to the production manager. He started to breathe easier in just a few moments after giving the injection. His pulse was racing from the epinephrine. I felt better about the entire situation, but he wasn't out of the woods by any stroke of imagination.

CHAPTER 42

The Wonder Drug

EPINEPHRINE (EP-*UH*-NEF-RIN, -REEN) is also known as adrenaline, a hormone. The effects are to provide energy so the major muscles of the body can respond to the perceived threat, a fight or flight response. Have you heard the term a hair-raising experience? Epinephrine has an effect on the smooth muscles in the body, causing a stimulation resulting in the contraction of the smooth muscle cells in the skin, resulting in the raising of the hairs on the surface of the skin. An injection of epinephrine also works to counteract the symptoms of anaphylaxis by opening the airways to reduce breathing difficulties and narrowing the blood vessels to combat low blood pressure and to ease the faint feelings. Epinephrine has a short half-life, so it is imperative to get the patient to a hospital immediately. All in all, it helps reverse cardiovascular collapse, which is real magic. No magic wand, spells, or incantations, Epinephrine is the real deal. There is no other medication on the face of the earth that acts on so many body systems at once. That is why epinephrine is the drug of choice for an anaphylactic reaction.

The history of epinephrine is interesting in that it was discovered by a Japanese chemist in 1900, Jo Kichi Takamine and his assistant, who independently discovered adrenaline. Then in 1901, Takamine successfully isolated and purified the hormone from the adrenal glands of sheep and oxen. Are you paying attention? This happened over a century ago. The airplane was still in the planning stages, along with hearing aids, air-conditioning, and the teddy bear. What you can accomplish by turning off your contact with social media, cellphones, and TV! I'm not saying cut them out completely, but look what else you can accomplish by turning those things off for periods of time in your life. I'm writing a book, for heaven's sake! The ambulance arrived in record time, and our crew member was safely transported to a local hospital. What a close call! I was very glad we were only filming at this location for the day. Everyone was glad to pack up and get back to the city.

CHAPTER 43

You Want My Number?

MOVING TO THE next location, Hugh arrived one morning and put a call in for the medic, me! He said he felt like he was getting the flu. Bummer. Especially when he's in every scene throughout the entire movie. He looked under the weather: peaked, muscles aching, and just plain tired. I don't have anything magical in my treatment bag, but I did have tea. Ginger tea to be specific. I've brewed a cup up for myself when I feeling "down under," and it worked wonders, along with staying in bed for twenty-four hours. Hugh didn't have that luxury, so I brewed him a cup of my best ginger tea and carried it over to the set where he was taking a break and talking to the director. I came around the corner where they were seated, face-to-face, across each other.

When I walked into the tent facing the director, he looked right up at me and said, "Can I have your phone number?"

I looked at him, and I looked at Hugh, then I looked back at the director and back at Hugh again and said, turning to Hugh and handing him the cup of tea, "I'm pretty sure he's talking to you. I know you're not feeling 100 percent well. Try this. I can't guarantee it'll work, but it's worth a shot." He did take the tea, smiled appreciatively, and thanked me.

"You know you're more than welcome," I said, smiling back at him. Hugh did make it through the entire day of filming, along with three more cups of my ginger tea! Want to know why the ginger tea worked so well? I'll put the answer to that in my next book!

CHAPTER 44

Fungoose Toeis

DAYS AND WEEKS of filming turned into months. Everyone on the crew was so familiar with each other. We were like family, making the otherwise mundane world I lived in a little brighter. Returning back to Detroit, we were greeted with thousands of extras on the set again. My radio never stopped ordering me around when we had that many extras. "Medic, Medic, Medic!"

To which I'd say out loud to the radio, as if it would listen to me, "That's my name. Don't wear it out!" Never knew what kind of ailments the extras would bring along with them to work from one day to the next. If they forgot their antibiotics, I sent them home. If they had a stuffy nose from allergies, I would bend the rule once in a while and give them an over-the-counter antihistamine.

Complaint of chest pain?" I would question the extra. "You have had chest pain since last Thursday, and you're just now bringing it to my attention five days later?" I contacted the PA to excuse them for the rest of the day, pay them for a day's work, put them in a cab, and send them to the hospital with a verbal instruction not to bother coming back to the set. Ever. Their days as an extra in this movie were over. I was always separating out the real complaints from "What in the world are you talking about?" complaints.

I came back from lunch one afternoon to find a very heavyset man sitting at my station with his sandals off and his feet propped up on my makeshift exam table. Really?

"Hi there, how can I help you?" I said, eyeing his dirty, dry, scaly feet.

"Well, I'm an extra, and last week I noticed I got this infection," he said, pointing to the big toe of his right foot. "I think I need to go to the hospital and have the doctor look at it since I got the infection here."

"Hmm," I said with feigned interest. "This could be very serious," I said as I put on a pair of gloves and donned a mask. I took ahold of his toe and inspected it from every angle. "Hmm, this is very interesting. Hang on." I took a magnifying glass out of my jump kit and looked at his toe intently. I turned the glass up, looking at him, knowing my eye would appear a hundred times its normal size through the glass. "My, my, my, this is quite an interesting case you have here."

"It is?"

"Yes, and I think you're right. You do need to go to the hospital and see a doctor."

"I do?" he sounded elated.

"Mm-hmm," I murmured on.

"What do I have?" He sounded so exhilarated at the mere mention of going to the hospital.

"Well...," I said, hanging on to his toe and cleaning it off with an alcohol wipe. "I call this fungoose toeis."

"What?" he said.

"Fungoose toeis," I repeated clearly and concisely. "I'll need to pull the nail off and send it to the ER and have their lab look at it to confirm my diagnosis. If it is 'fungoose toeis,' I'll have to send you to the ER to have your toe amputated. We'll cover the cost for everything. Don't you worry. We'll take good care of you!"

"Wait, wait, wait," he said. "Did you say you're going to remove my toenail?"

"Why, yes," I said, reaching over to my treatment bag, pulling out a hemostat and a surgical knife. "Don't worry. I can keep pressure on the wound so it doesn't bleed over everything until I receive the final report back from the ER. When I do get confirmation, we'll call an ambulance and send you right over to the ER and get your toe amputated."

"You what? You're going to amputate my toe?"

"No, not me," I said, laughing. "I'm just the medic. I'm only going to remove your toenail. The doctor does the amputations in the hospital. Don't worry. We'll pay you for your time here today. Okay, now let's get this started." He tried to pull his foot away from me.

"I really need to think this over first."

"What's there to think about?" I retorted. "You have an infection you say you got here on our movie set, so we need to treat it." I wouldn't let go of his toe. He wriggled in every direction, but I wouldn't let go. "Unless"—I paused—"there was a chance you actually got this 'infection' in your toes years ago. You took high school gym class, and in the showers after working out, you contracted what the doctors call onchomycosis or tinea unguium. I have a name for it called a fungus among us! A fungus infection in your toenails. I would venture a guess and say you've had this fungus in your toenails for twenty-five years or more, and nothing you've done to treat it has ever worked. How am I doing so far?" I added, judging by the thickness of the toenails, never letting go of his big toe.

He sat there totally speechless. I let go of his toe. "Now listen, and listen closely because I'm only going to say this once," I said, moving forward so my face was right in front of his. "Put your shoes back on your dirty feet with your fungus-filled toenails and get back to work. I never ever want to see you back at this medic station again for the duration of the movie. If I do, it will be the last time you ever work on any movie in the city of Detroit ever again. Got that?" He stood up, grabbed his shoes, and left. I thought, *Did he really think I was going to send him to the hospital and have his toe amputated? Really?*

CHAPTER 45

A Night Shoot I Will Never Forget

OUR DAY FILMING took a turn, and we began night filming down by the Detroit River near Cobo Hall. Ah, night shoots. I could live the rest of my natural life and never ever miss doing another night shoot. Your entire body metabolism gets turned upside down. For every week I do night shoots, it takes me the same amount of time to recoup. Like it or not, we were going to be shooting night scenes for the next two weeks with thousands of extras. I called in some extra help and settled in for a fortnight. Nothing spectacular happened. I received multiple calls over the radio, but between the extra help I had and myself, we were able to get through the duration of filming night scenes without any drama. Or so I thought.

Our night filming was coming to a close. Three more nights, and we would be done and going back to daytime filming and a normal life. I couldn't wait. It was just past 1:00 AM, and before dinner, when I received an urgent call over the radio. "Medic, Medic, Medic, what's your location?"

"Medic on 3. I'm right by the security station. Where's your emergency?" I said, grabbing my backpack.

"There's an extra in distress down by the riverfront less than a block east of security."

"I'm on it," I radioed back. I took off in a flash and came upon the most unusual scene. There was a young woman: early twenties, short, maybe five foot and around 250 pounds, wearing a strapless, above-the-knee, form-fitting black dress.

She was running around in a circle with a group of people standing by just watching her shake her hands in front of her face chanting, "I canna bereave! I canna bereave!"

"Wait, what is she saying?" I turned and asked security. He shook his head.

"I have no idea. She just keeps running in circles and keeps repeating 'I canna bereave, I canna bereave.'"

I thought at first, *Drugs? Did she overdose?* She just continued to run in a circle chanting, "I canna bereave, I canna bereave," continuing to shake her hands wildly in front of her face. I watched her for maybe thirty more seconds, and in "I canna bereave" time, it was like ten minutes. I stood in front of her, put my hands on her shoulders, and made her look at me.

"Stop!" I said. "Stop!" She stopped, totally caught off guard anyone would make her actually stop. She just stood there staring at me with tears welling up in her eyes. "What can't you believe?" She just had a desperate look in her eyes.

"I canna bereave!"

"What can't you believe?" I repeated. "You can't believe you're an extra in a movie? You can't believe you're in a movie with Hugh Jackman?" *Throw me a bone, something*, I thought.

"I canna bereave!" she repeated again and began to frantically run circles around me. She resumed her war chant, "I canna bereave," over and over and over again, so I continued to let her circle me several more times before I said, "Stop!" I stood back with my hands on her shoulders and looked at her.

"Are you saying you can't *believe* or you can't *breathe*?"

"Yes!" she shook her head.

"You can't breathe?" I confirmed. She kept shaking her head yes. *Why in God's name can't you breathe?* I thought. Then I looked down on her and said, very clearly, "Are you wearing Spanx?" She stood very still for the first time and answered yes. *Oh my god*, I thought. "Listen." I pointed to a porta-potty three feet away from us. "Go into that bathroom right now. Take off the Spanx and hand it to me through the door." She looked at me and walked to the bathroom, walked in, and closed the door. I waited just outside the door and thought for just another minute and knocked on the door and asked, "Are you also wearing a girdle?" It took her about twenty seconds, but she finally answered yes. "Take off the Spanx and the girdle and hand both of them to me through the door. Now. I don't care if you have to run around commando for the rest of the night, you're not wearing Spanx and a girdle anymore. Not tonight, not on my watch."

She came out several minutes later breathing without any difficulty. She sheepishly handed me the Spanx and the girdle, which was deposited immediately into a waiting plastic garment bag. Security wrote her name on the bag, and I assured her that when the extras were relieved for the day, just go to security, and they would return the items to her. I caught her by the shoulder when she was leaving and said, "Why in heaven's name were you wearing a Spanx and a girdle?"

"I know Hugh Jackman is the star of this movie, and I wanted to look good when he saw me," she said without missing a beat.

"You have to be kidding me. I worked with Mr. Jackman for six weeks before I even had a chance to get close enough to even say hi to him! You know he's a happily married man with children," I added. "What makes you think out of over three thousand extras here tonight, you'd even have a chance of meeting him? You know what, don't answer that. There is no sane answer to that question. But for the rest of the film, do *not* show up wearing Spanx and a girdle anymore! I would find out because I am the set medic for this movie. Now go back to work, relax, and just enjoy being an extra! Have fun." She smiled a little and went back to the set.

I canna bereave she did that. Spanx…, really?!

CHAPTER 46

Cracker Barrel and the Cracked Engine Block

I ENJOYED BEING AROUND the extras for the most part. Many of them were very creative in the way they spent their endless hours of downtime. Some brought classwork to finish, others knitted, and some played cards, anything to help wile away the time. I struck up a conversation with an elderly couple who said they had been selected to be extras in the last eight movies filmed in Detroit. Michiganders! They are the salt of the earth. Even during this stressful economic hardship, so many Michiganders found a way to get through it. Detroiters, I found, were especially gifted in the art of survival skills. It just made me so proud to be a Michigander and part of the movie industry who selected Detroit as a major city to film in.

Now the film crew was moving to yet another location in Detroit. I loved having the opportunity to see our great city, but it was certainly taking a toll on my van. One morning in particular, I was about twenty miles away from Detroit on the way into work when the engine overheat light came on. Steam started to pour out from under the hood of my car. I just managed to drive it over the ramp on Belleville Road off I-94. I had an 8:00 AM call time, and it was already 7:00 AM. "Oh no!" I said out loud. What am I going to do? They aren't supposed to start filming until the set medic is on-site, and with all the accidents this film had been plagued with since day 1, it wasn't just necessary but imperative the set medic be on site.

I telephoned a very dear friend who was a retired RN. She loved the excitement and chaos of a movie set only two thousand extras could provide. Lucky for me, she answered on the third ring and said this had better be good to get her up so early. I explained my emergent dilemma, and she said without a moment's hesitation, "I'm out the door."

"Wait! Remember, you're not allowed to take pictures or videos of anything on the set."

"Oh yeah, I remember you telling me that."

"Now go, get dressed, the clock is ticking! I'll get there as soon as I can. I really owe you big-time," I said to her. "Thank you so much!" I called security and explained what had happened and to provide a backup radio for my colleague who would be there around 8:15 AM.

Now I had to call a towing company, a rental car agency, and get some breakfast. Lucky for me, where I had broken down was only a ten-minute walk to a Cracker Barrel. *At the very least*, I thought, *I was going to have a good breakfast.* When life hands you lemons, make lemonade. In this case, my lemonade was going to be breakfast at Cracker Barrel. Yum! Cracker Barrel restaurant was a Michigan favorite and just a short walk away. I watched steam continue to pour out from under the hood of my van, totally out of commission. Well, I may as well get the eggs in a basket, fried apples, grits, and a large iced tea. My triglycerides were going to take a hit this morning, but I just didn't care. And I used the favorite phrase my colleague and friend Deb Howitt coined: "My care ability level was zero." The tow truck and car rental agency all arrived at the same time. My AAA card had not seen this much action in years. Emergency towing service and a discount on my car rent? Thank you, AAA!

CHAPTER 47

A New Van

I ARRIVED ON THE set around 1:00 PM. At first, I didn't give a lot of attention to all the concerns I was receiving from everyone. One of the transport drivers honked his horn at me when I walked by and yelled out the window, "Are you okay?" I gave him a thumbs-up.

"Van trouble!"

Everyone I ran into also voiced the same concern: "We missed you," "Are you okay?" "How's your van?" I wasn't used to this kind of attention at any time in my life. I was really touched by their sincere concern. I grabbed my medic backpack and headed off to the set and received a report from my friend who received a well-deserved hug of appreciation when I finally caught up with her.

"You saved me this morning! The van is going to cost a fortune, but I have a rental car to get by with until the repairs are completed. You didn't take any pictures or videos of anything or anyone, did you?"

She thought for a moment. "I like living on the edge, but I decided against it. What if this picture is nominated for the best picture at the Oscars? You're going to need a date, and I'm going to call you on the favor you owe me," she said, laughing.

"Hey," I replied, "there's always the chance we'll get nominated. Hollywood is full of surprises."

She got really close and whispered into my ear, "Did you ever find out what it was they are being so secretive about? I mean, why all the hush-hush? Why can't we take any pictures or videos? What are they protecting?"

I leaned back into her ear and said, "I did figure it out about a month or so ago."

"You did?"

"Yes, I did."

"Well, for the love of everything, tell me!"

I stared at her a long minute and then whispered back in her ear, "I just can't"—shaking my head—"I just can't."

"Why not?" she demanded.

"If I told you, I would have to kill you, and you're one of the few best friends I have, so no. I'm not going to tell you, but thanks for helping me out. Dinner maybe sometime soon? My treat."

"You think?" she answered back with a sarcastic grin. She packed her things and, several hugs from me later, was on her way.

I started to make my rounds. The radio was quiet. It seemed to know I needed some time to reorganize myself after the wicked morning I just had. I walked onto the set, and Taris was standing in the middle of the set working with the crew to get the lighting and angles just right before they called Hugh to film the next scene. According to the work board set up in the director's tent, we were two-thirds of the way done getting all the scenes scheduled filmed for the day. Taris saw me and waved, "G'day!" he yelled. I waved back, smiling, and walked over to one of the lighting trucks where Hugh was sitting on the tailgate, just killing time talking to some of the gaffers and cameramen waiting for the filming to start.

"Sandy!" Hugh said. "Hey!" I walked over to him.

"Hey yourself. How are you?"

"Me?" he said. "I'm not the one with a broken-down van. I heard what happened. You okay?" I was just touched by his concern.

"Yes, I'll survive."

"Anything I can do?" he asked. I thought for just a second, then I grabbed Hugh's shoulders with both hands and playfully shook him, and he being the consummate actor, fell right into character, letting his head bob and weave while I continued to shake him.

"You have gazillions of dollars, Hugh. Buy me a new van! My van just died!"

He looked at me, and I looked back at him, and we both started to laugh for a ridiculous amount of time—the ultimate stress releaser. Hugh looked at me and added, "Wouldn't a brand-new van with a big red bow make a great wrap gift at the postproduction party?"

"Oh, would it ever! You're such a tease! Thanks for making me laugh. I needed that. Need any tea?"

"No, I'm good," he said, and with a final smile and a wave, he was called to the set.

CHAPTER 48

The End is Near

NOW THE END of the film was imminent. You could feel the shift of the entire crew mentally and emotionally starting to get themselves psyched up for the wrap. Days, weeks, and months of working with Hugh was coming to a close. Outstretched hands with copies of all the different movies Hugh had been in were appearing for autographs. Hugh, being the consummate star, obliged by autographing each and every one of them during his breaks. His personal assistant had a stack of DVDs waiting for him with yellow sticky notes attached to each one, having requests to make it out to family and friends. I waited patiently until he signed all the DVDs for the day when I took mine up to him. It was a copy of *Someone Like You*, a movie he had starred in years earlier, one of my favorites and a total chick flick. No one does it better than Hugh. I had attached a yellow sticky note per protocol and handed him the DVD.

"Would you please sign this for me?" He took the DVD and read what was written on the sticky note and laughed. I asked him to write, "To Sandy, one of the best set medics I have ever worked with. Hugh." He looked at me and started to write. And he wrote and wrote. What was he writing? Not what I had scripted, which would have just taken thirty seconds. He looked up and saw me peering over his shoulder to see what he was writing and deliberately turned away and shielded what he was writing on the DVD. He finally finished, turned, and handed me the DVD.

"I'm guessing you're also going to want a picture with me?"

"Now what do you think?" I said just as playfully back to him. "I nearly sacrificed life and limb to get this gig so I could work on this movie just to meet you."

He laughed and said, "You know, I get that all the time." I handed his personal assistant my camera asking to please take several. I always blink. Hugh put his arm around my shoulder and pulled me in for a really nice shot. I could feel the hot tears welling up in my eyes. Hugh gave me a sweet hug and said, "Sandy, it's been a real pleasure."

"No, Hugh, the pleasure was all mine. I really had a great time working on this movie with you. A great story. Maybe I'll write a book about it!" I said back to him.

"You do that," he said.

The day marched on by, and I didn't receive one call on my radio. Not one. A new set record. Hugh stayed a little longer and posed for more pictures with the crew, shook hands, and then in a whirlwind of goodbyes, he was gone. I stood looking at the back of his transport SUV taking him away until I couldn't see it anymore. I walked back to my station and started to pack my things up. Security came by and offered to help me move all my gear to my newly repaired van. I stopped short of closing the last tote and saw the DVD he had signed for me. *What did he write?* I thought, looking at the DVD.

> To Sandy, the most incredible set medic in the entire world. I have never worked with anyone as wonderful as you.
>
> Be well,
> Hugh Jackman

I laughed until I cried. Life was not only good but, at this moment, really great! Hugh was not only a really gifted actor but a good sport. No wonder he was so well-liked.

CHAPTER 49

Time to Say Goodbye

THE CREW WAS breaking up. Some were flying back to LA; others were moving on to new set locations for filming in Toronto, New Orleans, or New York. There were so many different movie locations all happening at the same time. Some of the crew were staying behind in the Motor City to make another movie in Detroit. We all had a great time at the wrap party, which would have had a fantastic ending if I had arrived, and there was a brand-new van waiting for me. Hugh and his wife were always very generous at the close of every movie he stars in and didn't let the city of Detroit down. He and Mrs. Jackman dedicated a gift of money to a local women's domestic violence center who needed financial aid more than I would ever need a new van.

The crew feasted at a local restaurant in Greektown, which is a historical commercial and entertainment district in Detroit. This area was first settled in the 1830s by German immigrants who created a primarily residential neighborhood. However, in the earliest years of the twentieth century, most of the Germans were moving into areas farther from downtown, and Greek immigrants moved in, encouraged by the first documented Greek immigrant, Theodore Gerasimos. By the 1920s, the Greek immigrants were moving out of the residential spaces; but the restaurants, stores, and coffeehouses they established remained in the neighborhood. By the 1960s, the area was being commercially developed. The Greek leaders realized this culturally significant area was at risk. So they threw a Greek festival in 1966 coinciding with the Fourth of July. The festival was a huge success and continued for years. The Greektown area was firmly established in Detroit as the Greektown Historic District and has been listed on the National Register of Historic Places since 1982.

The movie crew feasted through the early morning hours to a constant stream of Greek music, feasting on *Amisia Paidakia*, a succulent Greek dish of marinated lamb chops grilled over an open fire, along with *Spanakoteropeta*, another Greek dish made up of fresh leaf spinach, imported feta cheese, and spices baked in thin delicate layers of phyllo dough. And how could any Greek meal be complete without *Moussaka*? Thinly sliced eggplant layered with potatoes, ground meat, and special spices baked with a beehamel custard and topped with tomato sauce, accompanied by platters of chicken, beef, and lamb kabobs grilled to perfection with plates of *Saganaki*. Flaming Greek Kasseri cheese topped with a blazing brandy and a resounding yell, "Opa!" The Greeks knew how to throw a party! And it was a great way to end production of the movie and see the entire crew and Hugh one more time!

CHAPTER 50

One Last Chance Meeting with Hugh

SEVERAL MONTHS LATER, I was out with friends, catching an early dinner at a local Detroit bistro, when my attention was drawn to the TV over the bar tuned into Oprah Winfrey. She was broadcasting live from Australia, featuring the major movie stars of that country. Nicole Kidman, Keith Urban, Russell Crowe, the "Crocodile Hunters," Terri, Bindi, and brother Robert Irwin were going to appear on stage with Hugh Jackman.

"Oh, look, everyone!" I said. "Hugh is going to be on Oprah!" They all stopped talking and came over to watch the excitement of seeing these movie legends and entertainers being welcomed to the stage during Oprah Winfrey's first visit to the Land Down Under. The show went on to describe the beautiful country of Australia and everything it had to offer. The crystal blue waters of the Great Barrier Reef, the Sydney Harbor Bridge and, of course, the stage they were performing on at the Sydney Opera House. One by one, Oprah introduced all her guests to the stage. I waited patiently for Hugh's name to be announced, and finally Oprah introduced him. The one, the only, Hugh Jackman. I looked to the side of the stage where I thought he was going to enter, but instead the camera panned up to an entrance high above the stage. The plan was for Hugh to zip line from the top sail of the opera house down to the stage. But while rappelling downward, doing roughly 80 km/h, Hugh hit the brakes too late and crashed onto the stage hitting his eye on a lighting rig in front of a packed opera house of six thousand loyal Oprah fans. You could have heard a pin drop. Then, clearly over the intercom, you could hear the announcement, "Medic, Medic, Medic! What's your location? Someone get the medic!"

I smiled and said out loud, "Medic on 3, I'm right here!"

The End

ABOUT THE AUTHOR

A GRADUATE OF UNLV with a BS in nursing, Sandy practiced and perfected her craft in emergency rooms and intensive care units across the country.

The opportunity to work as an RN set medic happened when she least expected it, but she embraced the novelty and uniqueness of working in the movie industry, where she met and medically treated world-renowned directors, producers, stagehands, and mega movie stars like Hugh Jackman.

Sandy continues to work as a nurse and write novels from her home in Ann Arbor, Michigan.